A fatal message . . .

Quivering, Cammi pointed out to sea.

Jessica looked into the distance. "There's nothing there," she said. Rats. *She'd hoped maybe it was a ship, set out to rescue them from the island. Still, it figured that one of Elizabeth's stupid friends would go around screaming for no good reason. She was turning back to Elizabeth when something else caught her eye. Something on the beach below the hill.*

"That's where we found the money," Elizabeth whispered. All the fight seemed to have gone out of her voice. Jessica shoved her aside impatiently and went to the edge of the hillside. She drew in her breath.

Etched carefully into the smooth, damp sand, in letters about eight feet high, was a message.

"A dollar sign," Jessica murmured, squinting to make sure she wasn't seeing things. Her eyes flicked over the rest of the writing. "OR YOU ARE—"

Oh, man. *Nervously Jessica licked her lips. "OR YOU ARE DEAD."*

SWEET VALLEY TWINS

Escape from Terror Island

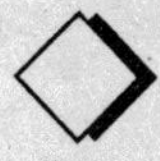

Written by
Jamie Suzanne

Created by
FRANCINE PASCAL

BANTAM BOOKS
NEW YORK • TORONTO • LONDON • SYDNEY • AUCKLAND

To Bradley Scott Halpern

RL 4, 008-012

ESCAPE FROM TERROR ISLAND
A Bantam Book / December 1995

Conceived by Francine Pascal

Produced by Daniel Weiss Associates, Inc.
33 West 17th Street
New York, NY 10011

Cover art by James Mathewuse

ISBN: 0-553-48195-9

Published simultaneously in the United States and Canada

Bantam Books are published by Bantam Books, a division of Bantam Doubleday Dell Publishing Group, Inc. Its trademark, consisting of the words "Bantam Books" and the portrayal of a rooster, is Registered in the U.S. Patent and Trademark Office and in other countries. Marca Registrada. Bantam Books, 1540 Broadway, New York, New York 10036.

PRINTED IN THE UNITED STATES OF AMERICA

OPM 0 9 8 7 6 5 4 3 2 1

One

Where was the boat? Elizabeth's heart pounded. Suddenly there was nothing around her, nothing but water—and the steady, ominous beating of the waves against the side of the Island Dreamer. I'm in the ocean, *she realized, struggling to keep calm.*

In the ocean, in the middle of a storm!

"Elizabeth!" Jessica and Todd were shouting, but by now their voices were nothing but thin, faraway ribbons of sound.

I've got to make it, *Elizabeth thought, a thread of panic rising in her stomach.* I've got to make it back to Jessica. *A ferocious swell of water swept over her head, and for terrifying moments she was sucked beneath the waves into the icy black ocean. Paddling furiously, she broke the surface again and gasped for breath. She couldn't keep this up much longer, she realized. It was still raining, and the ocean waves were tugging her ever downward and out to sea. Already her arms and legs were aching and tired, useless against the strength of the ocean.*

I've got to make it, *she thought wearily as she sank underwater again.* I've got to make it. *This time when she bobbed back to the surface, she could barely keep her eyes open. Suddenly, getting back to the boat seemed too difficult to try. She was OK where she was. Sleepily she blinked; she could no longer see the boat anyway, could no longer hear anyone calling her. Well, that was OK. Everything was OK. She was very, very tired and had to close her eyes just for a minute . . .*

The next time a wave washed over Elizabeth's head, spreading her long blond hair around her like a golden sunburst, she didn't struggle. There in the darkness of the ocean storm, she gave up the fight.

Kicking hard, Jessica Wakefield dragged her body through the churning water. *Elizabeth, where are you?* her mind screamed frantically. *Mandy, Lila—where is everybody?* Being on the pitching, rocking boat during the storm had been bad enough. But now that the boat had splintered in two and sunk out of sight, things were ten times worse.

Breaking the surface, Jessica took a deep mouthful of air. In the darkness and the pouring rain, she could barely see three feet in front of her. Her thoughts were a jumble. *Won't the storm ever stop?* she wondered desperately. *Can I stay afloat? Is there anything to grab on to?* She opened her mouth to scream, wondering whether she could be heard over the roar of the storm. But no sound came out.

Not knowing what else to do, Jessica began to swim. *The* Island Dreamer *can't be all gone, can it?* she wondered as she thrashed across the raging ocean.

There must be some pieces of wood left over—maybe I can grab one and rest—

Her arms felt very tired.

If only I'd stayed home, Jessica thought, remembering the events of that morning. Her mother, who had been supposed to chaperone the class field trip, had missed the boat, along with Mr. Seigel, their science teacher, and the other chaperones. *I could have stayed with them,* she thought miserably. *I was feeling a little sick last night. I should have just stayed in bed, and then—*

A huge wave smacked her in the face. Jessica sputtered and spat out the salty water. Before she could catch her breath, another wave pushed her beneath the surface. Once again Jessica kicked back up. Her legs ached. *I need to rest,* she thought miserably. *A piece of the ferry, another person, something, anything!*

Rain battered Jessica's head and shoulders as she gasped for breath. She reached her hand out into the darkness and felt—

Nothing.

Please, please, Jessica begged silently. *I'm so tired!* She knew she couldn't fight any longer. All she could do was try to keep her head above water. A bolt of lightning flashed nearby, followed by a mighty thunderclap. Terrified and exhausted, Jessica could feel her body go limp.

It's over, she thought, closing her eyes. *This is the end.*

And then even in her mind there was only blackness.

Elizabeth slowly opened her eyes and sat up. It was morning. Above her head stretched a warm blue sky. *Looks like a beautiful day,* Elizabeth told herself with a yawn. *Wow, I really slept well!*

She started to climb out of bed—and then realized she wasn't in bed at all.

"What's this sand doing here?" Elizabeth asked softly, running a handful through her fingers. "Now, why would I be sleeping on sand?"

She stood up, swaying a little unsteadily, and stared at her surroundings. "Wherever this is, it's beautiful," she murmured, rubbing her eyes.

In front of her a sandy beach extended about twenty yards down to the water. The ocean was a lovely azure blue. Little waves lapped gently against the clean white sand. A single seagull circled in the distance, and a gentle breeze caressed Elizabeth's face. "Everything's so peaceful," she said quietly, thinking about the crowds that usually jammed the beaches back home in Sweet Valley.

Wait a minute. Back home in Sweet Valley? Elizabeth blinked. *But if this isn't Sweet Valley, where else could it possibly be?*

Curious, Elizabeth looked all around her. To one side there were palm trees, swaying gracefully in the breeze. To the other, the beach continued, empty and inviting, as far as Elizabeth could see. The bright sunlight bathed the beach in a warm glow. Elizabeth breathed in deeply. The sea air was pure and fresh.

For a moment Elizabeth stood drinking in the air and listening. She couldn't remember ever being in a place so quiet. Besides her own breathing, the only noise she could hear came from directly behind her: a muffled burbling that sounded vaguely familiar. Walking a little way to investigate, she came upon a sparkling waterfall that cascaded down a rocky cliff and into a pool near the beach.

Elizabeth realized she was thirsty. Kneeling beside the pool, she filled her cupped hands with the glistening water. The water felt cool and looked clear. Taking a sip, she swished it around her mouth before swallowing. *Ah. It's perfect!* Elizabeth filled her hands again. "Heavenly," she murmured. Then a thought struck her. *Maybe this was heaven?*

Hmm. Elizabeth licked her lips and tried to think. Slowly she got to her feet, feeling an ache in her back. *Well, this can't be heaven, then,* she told herself. *In heaven people don't get sore. At least, I don't think they do. But if I'm not in heaven, then where am I?*

Something nagged at Elizabeth's memory. Something had happened last night. Something important. But she just couldn't remember what.

"Well, I'll ignore it for now," she murmured. *If it's really important, I'll remember it eventually,* she told herself. *And in the meantime I can enjoy this beautiful place.* She knelt down again, wincing a little, reached for some more water—and gasped.

A face was staring up at her from the clear calm waters of the pool.

Jessica! Elizabeth thought. A sinking feeling began to grow in her stomach. Elizabeth blinked and peered back into the water. "Bluish-green eyes," she muttered, her breath coming in gasps, "and long blond hair, and a dimple in the cheek—" It was her sister's face, all right.

Quickly Elizabeth thrust her hand into the water. *Jessica!* Her hand broke through the surface—and hit a rock about eight inches below. "Ouch!" she cried, pulling her arm back out.

With a start, she realized what had happened. *That was no real person's face,* she thought, scolding herself. *That was your own reflection.* "Of course," she said out loud, feeling embarrassed even though no one was around to see her. She stared at the water as the ripples began to vanish. Already she could see the reflected outlines of her own face. "Pretty silly," she muttered. "I'm so used to looking at Jessica's face, I can't even recognize my own anymore!"

Elizabeth tried to laugh. She looked around at the palm trees and the beautiful clear sky. But she couldn't enjoy the scenery the way she had a few minutes earlier. Something was gnawing at her. *Jessica,* she told herself, feeling a growing sense of worry. *Something about Jessica . . .*

All at once it came back to her. "The boat ride!" Elizabeth said, drawing in her breath. The storm suddenly became vivid in her mind. The boat lashed by waves, and the rain and wind whipping it back and forth, and then Elizabeth tumbling out into the sea below, and then—

And then—

But that was all she could remember. Shaking her head, Elizabeth looked around her. She could hardly believe that this peaceful place could be connected to that terrible storm. For a moment she wondered if she'd dreamed the whole thing. But no, her back hurt, her hair was a mess, and she'd woken up on the beach. She must have been washed up there during the night.

And where is Jessica? she thought, narrowing her

eyes. The restful quiet she had enjoyed a moment ago now seemed much more spooky. *Where is everybody? They were on that boat, too. Did they make it safely ashore, or—*

Elizabeth didn't dare think about that "or."

"Jessica?" she called softly.

There was no reply.

Elizabeth took a few steps back onto the beach. "Jessica?" she called again, a little louder this time. *Jessica, where are you?* Her heart beat faster. What if she was the only survivor?

"Jessica?" Elizabeth tried once more, her voice cracking with the effort. Her only answer was the cry of the seagull gliding far above the waves.

Fearfully, Elizabeth turned back toward the waterfall. *I guess I'd better have a look around,* she told herself woodenly. *Maybe Jessica got washed ashore someplace else on this—island.* If it was an island. *I'll just drink a little more water and then I'll look for her.*

Elizabeth took another sip. Then she stiffened. *What was that?*

Nearby, in the bushes, she heard a crackling sound.

Elizabeth wanted to call for Jessica, but she couldn't get any words out. Suddenly her mouth felt dry, though she'd just sipped some water. She stood up from the pool and peered nervously around a tree, holding her breath.

Two

"Elizabeth? Is that you?"

Elizabeth turned around at the sound of the familiar voice. "Amy!" Elizabeth exclaimed, running over to her friend Amy Sutton. "I thought—I thought—" She wrapped Amy in a hug. "I thought I was the only one here," she continued, her face buried in Amy's long, straight hair.

"I thought *I* was the only one here," Amy admitted. "When I heard you calling, I didn't know who it was, and, well—" She shrugged, looking embarrassed. "I was afraid to say anything."

Elizabeth stepped back and squeezed Amy's hand. "I kind of felt that way, too." Then she hesitated. "It really *is* you, isn't it?" she asked cautiously. "I mean, you're not, like, a mirage or anything, right?"

Amy's eyes twinkled. She reached out and pinched Elizabeth on the shoulder.

"Ow!" Elizabeth said. "What was that for?"

"Sorry," Amy said, suppressing a smile. "Just checking. I guess I'm not a mirage, after all."

"I guess not." Elizabeth grinned. "I wonder if there are others here—or if it's just us."

"I hope it's not just us," Amy said with a shiver. "We should probably go and look for the others—I mean, find the others."

"Oh, we'll find them all right," Elizabeth agreed with more confidence than she felt. "Let's have some water and go look—I mean, go find them."

Amy dropped to her knees and sipped from the pool. "This feels great," she said, pouring a little water over her hair to wash out some sand. "Which way should we go?"

Elizabeth looked around. One direction seemed about as good as any other. "You decide," she said at last.

Amy frowned and shook her head. "No, you."

Elizabeth took a deep breath. Who knew what was on the island in *any* direction? Then she thought of Jessica—no matter what, she had to find her sister. "Turn left," she said.

Squaring her shoulders, she and Amy headed down the beach together.

"This is one gorgeous place," Amy murmured a few minutes later. She darted forward and picked up a conch shell. "Look, Elizabeth. You don't find these on the beach in Sweet Valley very often!"

"No, you don't," Elizabeth agreed, examining Amy's shell closely. It was lovely, all right. She rolled it around her hand, enjoying the feel of the shell's smooth curves on her fingers. "How many different shades of pink do you think there are?"

Amy reached for the shell. "Three, four, five," she counted. "Six—no, wait a minute, I already counted that one." She smiled, gazing around as they passed a calm lagoon near the ocean's edge, surrounded by palm trees. "Look at that! It's like a *National Geographic* special or something. I bet there are some neat fish there, too."

"Probably," Elizabeth agreed. The idea of stopping to look was tempting, but she didn't dare. *I have to find Jessica,* she told herself. *That's the most important thing right now.*

They walked on for a couple of minutes. "Elizabeth?" Amy asked at last, her voice breaking the stillness.

Elizabeth turned to look at her friend. "What is it?"

"I'm just feeling nervous," Amy confessed. "I'm—I'm—" She swallowed hard. "Do you see the way the beach is curving around? It makes me think we're on an island, and if we're on an island—then we would need a boat to get off," she finished in a very small voice.

"I'm nervous, too," Elizabeth admitted, reaching for Amy's hand. "But I'm sure we'll figure out something. And I'm *positive* we'll find the others," she went on, crossing her fingers behind her back. "They must be here somewhere."

"I hope you're right."

"Of course I'm right," Elizabeth told her, trying to sound as carefree as possible. She wondered if Amy had noticed how smooth and free of footprints the beach was. No one had walked along this stretch of sand. Not for a long time anyway. Elizabeth hastily pushed these thoughts to the back of her mind. "I know!" she said. "Let's take off our shoes. Maybe it'll feel like an ordinary walk along the beach."

She realized that her feet had been through a lot lately. She'd gotten a splinter on the ferry when she'd temporarily lost one of her shoes. And now her feet were soaking wet in her sneakers. It would feel good to walk along the warm sand.

Amy nodded. "Good idea," she said, slipping off her sneakers. Tying the laces together, she draped her shoes over her neck. "You're right," she called back to Elizabeth as she waded into the sea. "This feels a lot better."

Elizabeth took off her own shoes and tied them the way Amy had. She dug her toes into the warm sand. Closing her eyes, she concentrated on feeling peaceful and rested. *It's just an ordinary day at the beach,* she told herself, remembering how visits to the beach usually relaxed her. *Where's the sun?* Elizabeth turned till the sunlight shined directly at her. *There.* Her feet grazed something smooth. *A rock,* Elizabeth guessed. She strained to identify the sounds around her. *That's a palm tree rustling in the breeze,* she told herself. *That's Amy splashing in the water—that's a seagull. And that one—*

Confused, Elizabeth scrunched her eyes tighter. *That one—*

"Hey!"

Elizabeth's eyes flew open. *That's a human voice!* she thought with delight just as she heard Amy cry out, "Maria!" There, coming out of the forest, was a group of kids: Maria Slater, Todd Wilkins, Randy Mason, Cammi Adams, and several others. They looked tired and bedraggled, but Elizabeth's heart leaped as they came near. "Hi, guys!" she said happily, running to meet them, her tennis shoes bouncing on their strings.

"Elizabeth!" Maria greeted her with a hug. "We've been looking all over for you! Where have you been?"

"Down that way." Elizabeth pointed. "There's a waterfall with a little pool at the bottom and water to drink—and *we* were looking for *you*."

"Water, huh?" Todd said, licking his lips. "We picked a couple of melons and shared them, but I'm kind of thirsty."

"Me too," Maria added. "Let's go!"

"Wait a minute," Elizabeth said anxiously. "Have you seen anybody else?"

"Anybody else?" Randy Mason looked blank.

"Like—Jessica, for instance?" Elizabeth ventured, suspecting that she already knew the answer.

"Oh, Jessica." Maria wrinkled her nose and reached out to pat Elizabeth's shoulder. "No, I'm sorry. We haven't seen anybody else all morning."

"Oh." Elizabeth bit her lip.

"We haven't gone very far," Cammi Adams added quickly. "There's a whole bunch of places we haven't looked. Maybe she's in the forest?"

"Maybe," Elizabeth said slowly, hoping Cammi was right.

"Can we go to the waterfall now?" Todd asked, dropping a melon rind on the beach. "I'm really thirsty."

Elizabeth hesitated, staring into the dense woods. Part of her wanted to go with her friends. But another part of her wanted to search the woods for her sister. "Well, I—"

"Come with us, Elizabeth," Amy urged, gently steering Elizabeth down the beach. "You don't want to go into that forest all alone."

Elizabeth glanced at her friend. *Amy's right,* she thought. The woods did seem a little ominous. Reluctantly she let her friend guide her back the way they'd come. *I don't want to go looking for Jessica all by myself—*

What I really want is for Jessica to come out here looking for me!

I'm dreaming, Jessica told herself as she wandered through the forest. *Birds are singing, it's a perfect day for a tan, the sky is an awesome shade of blue—and whenever I want something to eat, I pick a piece of fruit and dig in!*

Smiling, she held her face up to the sunlight. *Any minute now I'll wake up,* she thought, *and I'll regret it for the rest of my life.* "It *has* to be a dream," she said out loud, her voice echoing in the silence around her. "Because it's too good to be true."

Walking on, Jessica strained to memorize all the details of this beautiful place. She hated it when she woke up and couldn't quite recall everything she'd dreamed about. "All this place needs is a beach," she thought. She could picture it in her mind. A beautiful, white, sandy beach, deserted and inviting, stretching as far as she could see, the sand sparkling in the sunlight, the bluish-green ocean waters matching the color of her own eyes—

Jessica paused. Somehow that beach seemed awfully real. Almost as though she'd actually seen it.

"Well, anything can happen in a dream," Jessica reminded herself. Still, she felt a prickling sensation in her stomach. *Of course this is a dream—isn't it?*

Jessica picked another melon, peeled back the rind, and bit in. *Mmmm. You'd never eat anything this delicious in real life,* she reasoned, letting the juice drip down her chin. "And if this were real life," she added thoughtfully as she chewed, "Mom'd make me wipe my face—"

"Jessica!"

Startled, Jessica looked up—to find herself staring at her friend Lila Fowler.

Or something that looked a lot like Lila, anyway. Jessica frowned and rubbed her eyes. Lila cared more about her appearance than anyone Jessica knew—herself included. But here was Lila—or this thing that looked like Lila—in a torn purple sweatshirt, her hair matted, her cheeks scratched and puffy. Jessica tried hard to suppress a shudder. "You look terrible," she said, curling her upper lip. *That's the best thing about a dream,* she told herself cheerfully. *You can be completely honest with your friends.*

Lila stared back. "Like you're not having a bad hair day yourself," she retorted. "Besides, I don't see what *you're* doing in my dream."

"*Your* dream?" Jessica was outraged. "What are you talking about? This is *my* dream." *And you have no business barging into it!*

"I beg your pardon," Lila said haughtily, "but this dream is mine. I could wake up any minute and you'd be history. Poof!" She snapped her fingers. As she did, Jessica noticed that the tips of Lila's prized fingernails had broken off.

"Yeah, right," Jessica sneered. "I got here first, so

it's my dream— Hey!" An idea had just occurred to her. "Maybe this dream is, like, both of ours."

"You mean we're sharing it?" Lila looked doubtful.

"Sure." Jessica sat down on a log. "Listen. In your dream, what color are those berries?" She pointed.

Lila glanced at the bush. "Blue."

"Same here," Jessica said, growing excited. *This is cool!* she thought. *I wonder if we'll remember this tomorrow at school.* "Now it's your turn. Ask me something."

"Um—what are you sitting on?" Lila said.

"A log!" Jessica looked down. "It's brownish-grayish and kind of hollow—"

"Oh, wow," Lila said slowly. "This is so weird."

"We probably have ESP or something," Jessica added. "Hey—" She swallowed hard. "Is there a beach in your dream, too? A long white sandy beach next to the ocean? With palm trees all around?"

"Oh, my gosh!" Lila cried. She reached for Jessica's hand. "Yes. Yes. And—and seashells. And bluish-greenish water. And—"

Jessica's whole body seemed to be tingling. "Mine too," she said, forcing herself to remain calm. "Water the same color as my eyes, right?"

Lila peered closely at Jessica. "Well—not really," she said after a moment. "Your eyes are more kind of hazel."

"They are not!" Jessica glared at her friend. "They're bluish-green, just exactly like the water."

Lila rolled her eyes. "Sure they are. Nice try, Jessica."

Jessica put her hands on her hips. "Well, if that's what you think, you can just get out of my dream!"

"Oh, yeah?" Lila took a step forward. "You listen to me—"

But she never finished her sentence. "Jessica! Lila!" came a familiar voice. Bruce Patman walked into the clearing. He was followed by Aaron Dallas, Jessica's sort-of boyfriend, Janet Howell, Mandy Miller, and a few other kids. *They look even worse than Lila,* Jessica thought.

"Thank goodness!" Janet Howell wiped her forehead and sighed dramatically. Janet was an eighth-grader and president of the Unicorn Club, an exclusive group of popular girls at Sweet Valley Middle School to which Jessica and Lila belonged. Janet was hanging on Bruce's arm. "I was *so* worried."

"What are you talking about?" Jessica asked, frowning.

"We thought you were lost," Aaron explained.

"Of course I wasn't." *Really, how could they all be so dense?* "How could I be lost in *my* dream? I mean, you're just figments of my imagination, that's all."

"You mean of *my* imagination," Lila hissed in her ear.

"Whatever." Honestly, this was the weirdest dream she'd ever had.

"What's all this stuff about dreams?" Bruce demanded, looking from Jessica to Lila and back.

Janet sighed loudly. "Oh, what difference does it make?" she said. "Lila! Jessica! The most amazing thing just happened! Bruce Patman risked his own life." She paused and batted her eyelashes. "To save mine!"

"No kidding?" Jessica asked, surprised. Even for a dream, that sounded pretty weird. Bruce Patman was by far the most gorgeous guy at school, but he was usually a jerk. "The Bruce Patman I know wouldn't risk his life to save anybody," she argued.

Bruce and Janet glared at her.

"I think it was kind of by accident," Mandy Miller whispered. "She fell off a rock and landed on him."

Janet glared at Mandy. "You may be a Unicorn, but you're just a sixth-grader. You wouldn't understand," she said loftily. She gazed dreamily at Bruce. "Can you imagine! Not only cute. But strong and brave, too."

"In *my* dream?" Jessica asked. This was getting stranger by the minute.

"Who cares about dreams?" Janet said, sounding annoyed. She turned back to Lila. "Whatever Bruce says, goes." She poked Bruce. "Right, Bruce?"

"Uh-huh," Bruce said importantly.

"So what's this about dreams, Jessica?" Mandy asked curiously.

Aaron narrowed his eyes. "Maybe she hit her head real hard during the accident," he suggested. "Lots of times people do that and lose their memories. I saw a show about it on TV."

The accident? There was that prickling feeling again. Something was on the tip of Jessica's tongue—if she could only figure it out—

"I bet you're right." Mandy turned to Jessica. "Remember?" she asked gently. "We were on a field trip, and the ferryboat was hijacked by a couple of robbers, and then there was a storm? Thunder and lightning, remember?"

Lightning! Jessica's eyes snapped wide open. With the speed of a lightning bolt, the day before suddenly flashed back into her mind. The storm split the little ferry into matchsticks, and she was washed ashore onto the beach she thought she'd dreamed.

"So it *was* real," Jessica said softly. She looked around the group in front of her. "And you're real, too."

"Duh hey." Bruce rolled his eyes.

"Obviously." Janet sniffed.

"And we have to find Elizabeth," Jessica went on, thinking out loud. Her heart skipped a beat. *What if—*

"So what are we going to do next?" Aaron asked, sitting on the log.

"Well, we need water," Mandy pointed out.

"Why don't you listen to what Bruce has to say?" Janet demanded.

"We need to send out scouting parties," Bruce announced. "That's the only sensible thing to do."

"Water." Jessica realized that she was thirsty. "I think Mandy's right."

"Who cares?" Bruce said rudely. "Let's see. Lila and Aaron, you go that way." He gestured with his thumb. "Janet and I will cover—"

"But there might be lions and tigers," Lila cut in, frowning. "We should all stick together."

Bruce folded his arms, looking impatient. "There aren't any lions or tigers in California."

"How do you know we're still in California?" Lila demanded. "Who knows how far the storm pushed us before the boat sank?"

"Or how far the current carried us after that?" Jessica chimed in, still worried about Elizabeth.

"And anyway," Lila added before Bruce could speak, "California might not have lions, but it does have bears. Fierce, wild bears. I'm not walking

Three

"This is the life!" Maria said happily as they headed down the beach toward the waterfall. "Plenty of fruit, running water, a beautiful sky—what more could you want?"

Well, Jessica for one thing, Elizabeth thought.

"I know what you mean," Cammi agreed, stooping to pick up a smooth black rock from the beach. "There's something really neat about living on a desert island."

Randy frowned. "Are we sure this is an island?" he asked.

"Well—" Maria said thoughtfully. "The beach seems awfully empty. If we were on the mainland, wouldn't there be roads?" She jumped to avoid a wave. "I mean, think about all the things the Sweet Valley beaches have that they don't have here."

"Hot-dog stands," Cammi said with a smile.

"Lifeguard stations," Todd suggested. "Volleyball

nets." He grinned at Elizabeth. "Leftover sandwich wrappers and paper cups from picnics."

"Yuck," Elizabeth said, wrinkling her nose.

"You're probably right, Maria." Amy nodded. "You know what this place reminds me of?" she asked suddenly, drawing a line in the sand with her big toe.

"What?" Elizabeth turned toward her friend.

"Do you remember the book *Island of the Blue Dolphins*?" Amy asked. Her face clouded over. "The one about the native girl who lived alone on an island? We read it in school last year."

"Uh-huh," Elizabeth replied. She remembered the book well. When the rest of her tribe had moved to the mainland, the girl had been left behind with only her dog for company. "It happened around here, didn't it?"

"That's right." Amy bit her lip thoughtfully. "What if this place isn't as empty as we think? Maybe there are people in the forests somewhere. Indians with spears and poison-tipped arrows—a tribe that no one ever found."

"Poison-tipped—arrows?" Todd repeated.

"Oh, come on, you guys," Elizabeth protested. "If there were any natives, they'd probably be pretty gentle. Most of the California Indians were."

"Hey, what's that moving up there?" Cammi asked, shading her eyes.

"Just a tree branch," Elizabeth said impatiently.

Amy gasped. "Or maybe—maybe the people who made it here never made it back." She swallowed hard. "If you know what I mean."

Todd drew back in alarm. "Cannibals?" he half whispered.

"Don't be silly." Elizabeth reached for his hand. "The California Indians weren't cannibals." She gave a little laugh, hoping she sounded convincing. Deep down, though, Elizabeth's stomach was churning. *Jessica,* she found herself thinking. *Jessica—on an island with cannibals—*

Then she shook her head. The idea was ridiculous.

"Well, maybe there aren't any *cannibals* exactly, but I read this book about pirates who came to an island and just—stayed," Maria said, twisting the sleeve of her T-shirt. "Their descendants are still living there. You don't suppose—"

"It could be," Cammi said, looking down at the black rock she'd picked up earlier. "Oh, my goodness!"

"What is it?" Elizabeth asked, leaning forward.

"This rock," Cammi said, turning it around in her fingers. "It looks almost like a small cannonball."

"It does look like a cannonball," Elizabeth agreed. She reached out and stroked the smooth, worn sides. "It looks like—like a cannonball that's been in the water for years and years and years," she said slowly, looking up at Cammi's face.

"It sure does," Todd agreed. He licked his lips and gazed off to sea. "Guess I'll watch out for some pirate sails," he murmured.

A thrill of fear went up Elizabeth's spine. "They could be gentle by now," she argued without much conviction.

"No, they couldn't," Maria said flatly. "Once a pirate, always a pirate."

"Aren't we kind of visible here on the beach?" Amy asked. "If there really are pirates, or cannibals, or anything else, I'd rather be in the forest where we can hide." She glanced around. "We're too easy to see here. They can swoop down on us and we'd be—" Her voice trailed off.

"Dead meat," Todd finished for her.

"Uh-huh." Amy nodded grimly.

"But—" Elizabeth began. *There can't be any pirates or cannibals here,* she thought furiously. *There can't be!* She only wished she could believe it. Though the sun was still shining, Elizabeth suddenly felt as if the temperature had dropped twenty degrees. She shivered.

"So we should go inland," Maria said. She turned to Amy. "Can you find the waterfall through the woods?"

Amy took a deep breath. "I think so."

"Then that's what we'll do," Maria said.

Elizabeth peered suspiciously into the forest. Was that something moving or just her imagination? *Probably my imagination,* she told herself. *But still—*

She turned to Cammi. "When I say 'now,'" she hissed, her voice dropping to a whisper, "throw your cannonball, I mean your *rock,* into that clump of trees. OK?"

"OK," Cammi hissed back. "Why?"

"Just—just in case." Elizabeth silently counted to three. "Now!"

Cammi let fly. The rock arched up into the clear sky, a dark speck against the blue background. Elizabeth watched it land between the trees with a dull thump.

There was complete silence.

"Nothing," Elizabeth said at last. Her throat felt dry. *It's not like I expected to see anything,* she told herself, *but still—better safe than sorry.*

Taking a deep breath, she followed Amy into the forest.

What was that? Jessica seized Lila's hand. "Did you hear something?" she asked in a hoarse whisper.

Lila nodded. Her face was pale. "A thumping noise," she whispered back.

She heard it, too, Jessica thought, feeling faint. The noise had come from a clump of trees beside the path. "A lion," she muttered, struggling to get a grip on herself. *Thump, thump, thump.* The sound echoed in her brain. *Just exactly the noise made by a hungry lion loping across the plain after an antelope—*

Or after—

Jessica squeezed her eyes shut tight. She didn't want to think about it.

Mandy tapped Lila on the shoulder. "It's a great ape swinging down from a vine," she said in a panicky voice. "Remember those old Tarzan movies?"

"Don't." Lila gasped. Her knees began to sway.

Jessica looked to Bruce for reassurance, but Bruce didn't look very reassuring. He stood stock-still, his mouth a thin red line, his eyes darting back and forth anxiously. "So what are you staring at, Wakefield?" he demanded when he caught sight of her.

"N-nothing," Jessica told him, quickly looking away. *Some tough guy!* she thought. "Let's get out of here," she muttered.

"Uh-huh." Aaron took a step back.

Jessica put one foot slowly behind her, twisting to make sure nothing was blocking her path. Then she transferred her weight. Staying calm was hard work, especially with visions of lions dancing in her head.

"Let's hurry," Lila whimpered. She turned to run.

"No!" Jessica pulled hard to stop her friend. Their sweaty palms almost slid apart, but Jessica held on. "Don't you see? If you run, the wild animals will hear us."

"Oh!" Lila squeaked.

Bruce glared over his shoulder at them. "Quiet!" he mouthed.

Jessica rolled her eyes. "Yes, sir!" she whispered back, saluting.

Backwards they went. All was quiet, which made Jessica think about tigers. *Can't tigers walk forever without making noise?* Lila was clutching her hand so tightly, Jessica worried her fingers would break.

Backwards, always backwards. Jessica found herself making up a rhyme about what she was doing: *One, put your foot back; two, check for sticks; three, put your weight down; four, five, six.* Jessica said it in her mind over and over. *Pretty stupid,* she told herself. But it helped keep her mind off the animals.

They had gone about a hundred yards when Bruce halted, his eyes flashing. "Bunch of wimps!" he whispered. "There's obviously nothing here."

Jessica frowned. "Then why are you whispering?"

Bruce gave her a piercing look, then reached down and picked up a couple of broken, jagged sticks. Licking his lips, he handed one to Aaron and kept the other for himself. "Let's go," he hissed, taking a step forward.

"What's the deal with the stick?" Jessica asked. "To protect yourself from things that don't exist?"

"Quiet, Wakefield!" Bruce responded, looking away.

Jessica snorted impatiently. *Well, two can play that*

game! Bending down, she grabbed a long stick from the ground and broke it smartly over her knee. The crack sounded like a pistol shot.

Aaron jumped. "Hey, what's the idea?" he demanded in a whisper.

"Why don't you ask Bruce?" Jessica suggested, handing half the stick to Mandy.

Elizabeth gasped. *What was that cracking noise?*

"You see?" Maria muttered darkly. "There are *too* people on this island."

"That sounded almost like a gunshot," Todd said in a faint whisper. "Maybe we ought to, you know, lie down and hide."

"Maybe," Cammi said miserably, gnawing on the end of her fingernail.

"We need to get out of here, that's for sure." Nervously, Elizabeth wiped a strand of hair away from her forehead.

"But where?" Amy asked.

Elizabeth glanced around the group, only to realize that everyone was waiting for her to speak. "I guess to the waterfall," she said slowly. "Yes. There's water," she continued a little more firmly, "and maybe we can hide among the rocks."

"Anything's better than this." Cammi looked at the trees around her and shuddered. "I feel all closed in, know what I mean?"

Elizabeth knew, all right. Slowly they picked their way over rocks and logs, trying not to make a sound. "That's quicksand," she heard Randy mutter as Amy led the group around a wet spot. Elizabeth shivered. *I'll be awfully glad to get off this island!* she thought.

She breathed a sigh of relief when at last the trees opened up and the waterfall came into view.

"This is really awesome," Maria said, reaching out to touch the spray.

"There's a ledge we can stand on," Elizabeth said, pointing near the base of the falls. "Let's wait there for a while and see what happens."

Todd nodded. "Good thinking."

Elizabeth led the way onto the ledge, which snaked slowly up the side of the cliff. *This really is a good place to hide,* she thought. *The falls block the ledge so it's hard to see.* Elizabeth looked up the cliff that towered above her. "I don't think they'll be able to see us from above, either," she murmured hopefully, wondering whether "they" were pirates or something else—*something worse.*

The path came to an end right beside the falls. Elizabeth could feel the spray on her face. She looked down into the churning water. *About five feet above the pool,* she guessed, steadying herself against Amy's shoulder.

The other kids were all on the ledge by now, crowding together toward the falls. Elizabeth crouched down, her back to the cliff.

Her fingers closed around a rock. *Just in case,* she told herself.

It made her feel better to have a weapon.

Sticks at the ready, Jessica and her group climbed a hillside. Jessica was remembering a movie she'd seen where a bunch of kids attacked a wild boar with sharpened sticks. *I hope mine's sharp enough,* she thought.

Do they have boars in California?

"Water!" Mandy's whisper broke the silence. Ahead of them a stream was flowing swiftly down the hill. Mandy dropped to her knees and drank deeply.

"Is it good?" Janet came closer.

"Terrific." Mandy scooped another handful into her mouth as the others joined her. "Can you hear the waterfall?" she asked.

"What?" Jessica splashed a little water on her face. *What a great invention water was,* she thought.

"A waterfall. I think." Mandy narrowed her eyes and strained to hear.

"You mean you guys can't hear it?" Bruce snickered. "It's kind of obvious. I heard it way back at the bottom of the hill." His voice grew firm. "Drink what you want and let's get going."

"How come?" Jessica sat up and stared at Bruce.

"Because—" Bruce frowned. "Because where there's a waterfall, there's a pool," he said, looking embarrassed. "And where there's a pool, there are probably—" He stopped short.

Wild animals, Jessica finished in her head. She stood up. "You're right, Bruce. We'd better go." Splashing across the stream, she and Mandy headed down the other side of the hill.

"I didn't drink all I wanted!" Lila complained, tagging along. "I'm on a very important diet that says I have to drink twelve glasses of water a day and—"

"Do you want to be eaten alive by elephants?" Aaron demanded, grabbing Lila's hand and pushing her forward.

Mandy turned around. "Lila," she began, "if you want to stay here all by yourself—" But she never finished her sentence. A look of panic came suddenly into her eyes.

To her shock, Jessica saw the ground give way beneath Mandy's feet. She made a grab for her friend's hand, but missed.

"Mandy!" Jessica wailed as the girl disappeared into the earth.

Four

"We're doomed!" Maria cried.

Todd's face was white as a sheet as he huddled closer to Cammi on the ledge. "It's all over now," he muttered.

Elizabeth whirled around to face Amy. She could feel the blood pounding through her head, keeping time with the rhythm of the waterfall. "Did you hear that, too?" she whispered, tightening her grip on the rock in her hand. *Tell me it was only the cry of a seagull,* she begged Amy silently.

"It was definitely human," Amy said sadly. "The word was, 'Maa-daa!' It's probably a cannibal language."

"The beginning of a ceremony where they eat their captives," Randy said, moving toward the waterfall. "I saw a documentary on it last munch—" He shook his head violently. "I mean, last *month*."

"I thought it was a pirate war cry," Maria said

helplessly. "He said, 'Bang-dee!' It's an old way of saying 'Attack!' I think. Didn't you hear 'Bang-dee,' Cammi?"

Over the roar of the waterfall, Elizabeth could hear Cammi whimper.

"Whatever," Elizabeth said. "Either way, we're in big trouble." *I've never heard anything like it before,* she thought, shifting position as Cammi pressed toward her. "I guess we can only hope they don't see us and—hey! Don't push!"

But it was too late. In their haste to reach the very edge of the waterfall, Randy and Cammi had knocked the whole line off balance. Elizabeth felt herself teetering over the rim of the cliff. She tried to stretch forward, but the pull backwards was too strong. Frantically she reached out for Amy's shirt. Her hand grabbed once, twice, three times—and touched nothing but air. And then Amy's startled face was above her and there was a scream, which, she thought vaguely, might be her own—and then there was nothing but water, water pouring down in torrents onto her head as the pool rushed up to meet her—

And then there was nothing at all.

"Mandy? Mandy?"

Fighting a sense of panic, Jessica threw herself to the ground. *She can't have gone far,* she thought. *I mean, she was here a minute ago. Wasn't she?*

"Mandy!" Jessica peered through the broken earth.

"I'm here!" Mandy's voice floated up. "I think I've fallen into a pit or something." She sounded shaken but unhurt. "My foot hit some loose soil and the bottom just fell out from under me."

"Some people will do anything to get attention," Janet muttered to Lila.

"How far down are you?" Jessica called. Anxiously she reached her arm down into the pit, trying not to think about wild animals. "Can you see my arm?"

"A little. I'm standing on tiptoe," Mandy told her. "Do you think you can get me out?"

Jessica's heart had slowed back to normal. She took a deep breath. "We can try," she said, wriggling forward. "What's it like down there, anyway?"

"Not bad," Mandy answered. "There's a little bit of light, and the ground is covered with dry leaves."

"I knew it!" Jessica said. "It's probably a tiger's den."

Bruce sighed. "There aren't any tigers on this island, Wakefield," he said, sounding annoyed. "We've already been through all that. If you don't want to help Mandy out, then I will. Move aside." He set his stick down and knelt beside Jessica. "Here, Mandy. Grab my hand."

"Some people will do anything to hold Bruce Patman's hand," Lila said to Janet. "Isn't it pathetic?"

Jessica rolled her eyes. *I know Bruce is amazingly gorgeous,* she thought, *but I seriously doubt that Mandy fell into that hole just so—*

Just then an unearthly cry shattered the stillness. Jessica's blood froze.

"Oh, man," Bruce said slowly, licking his lips.

"It's on the other side of the hill," Aaron said, grabbing his stick tighter. "It's—it's—it's the hunting cry of the cougar." Little beads of perspiration were breaking out on his forehead. His breathing had become quick and shallow.

"No, it's not," Jessica said miserably. "It's a humongous bird announcing that it's found a victim." Her eyes drifted upward.

"A bird?" Lila repeated, looking panicked. "How big exactly?"

Jessica tried to think. "Big," she said. "Way bigger than an eagle. It was in the video we saw last year about native vultures of California—I mean, native *cultures*."

"Vultures?" Lila repeated in horror.

"Out of my way!" Janet gave Jessica a hard shove from behind. Jessica tumbled down into the pit and landed on her shoulder with a thump.

"Ow!" Mandy cried. "You landed on my foot!"

"Sor-ry," Jessica grumbled, picking herself up. "I think it's raining people." One by one, the others jumped down into the pit. It was a tight squeeze, and Jessica's shoulder ached. But as her eyes became accustomed to the darkness, she had only one thought.

Better down here—than up there!

Elizabeth snapped her eyes open. *Where am I?* she wondered.

The sky was there, all right, but fuzzy, almost as though she were looking at it through a glass bottle. Nearby were greenish rocks. There was a terrible pounding in her ears. She opened her mouth to breathe—and choked violently. *Water!*

I'm under the waterfall, Elizabeth realized with a start. *That's algae on the rocks, and the sky looks distorted because it is, and—*

And I have to get some air or I'll die.

Elizabeth stroked back up toward the surface of the pool. It was deep—much deeper than she had expected. No matter how hard she pushed, she couldn't seem to make much headway. She felt her arms grow tired, and her lungs seemed to be on fire—yet no matter how hard she struggled, the sky came no closer.

It's the waterfall, she told herself. *Of course! The waterfall is pushing me down, and it's too strong for me.* With her last ounce of strength, Elizabeth swam blindly along the bottom of the pool. Two strokes—three—four. *I should be out from under the falls by now,* she thought, trying hard to ignore the searing pain in her chest. *How long can you hold your breath, anyway?* She turned and headed straight up. Higher—higher—*ah.* Elizabeth broke the surface and gasped deeply. She'd never been so happy to feel fresh air on her face.

Treading water, Elizabeth looked around. "I'm behind the falls," she said wonderingly, taking another shuddering breath. "Hey—this is great!"

Elizabeth was in a little backwater. On one side the falls came down in a solid sheet of water. On two other sides, rock faces formed a ceiling over her head. And on the fourth side, directly in front of her, was absolutely the most awesome sight Elizabeth had ever seen—

A cave.

A dry cave, just a foot or so above the surface of the pool. Elizabeth swam to the side and hoisted herself out. *A perfect hiding place!* Best of all, a narrow passage led to the ledge where the rest of the group was sitting. She could see Amy's back. *They won't have to come in the way I did,* Elizabeth thought, squeezing water out of her clothes. An old riddle jumped into her mind.

What do you get when you swim under Niagara Falls? Elizabeth asked herself with a rueful grin, a puddle collecting by her feet.

Wet!

"This is a really terrific place, Elizabeth," Maria said a few minutes later. The kids were wedged together in the mouth of the cave, staring at the shimmering waterfall in front of them.

"I can't believe anyone could ever find us here," Cammi said confidently.

"I hope you're right." Elizabeth decided not to mention that sooner or later they would have to go back out to look for Jessica. And to find food. She tried to ignore the dull ache of loneliness in the pit of her stomach. She wished she could feel safe and content like Cammi. But she just couldn't.

"It really is almost completely dry in here," Amy said, touching the rock walls of the cave. "You'd think it would be all wet and muddy, but it isn't."

"I know what you mean." Maria looked behind her. "How far back do you think this cave goes, anyway?" she asked, staring into the half-darkness.

Reluctantly Elizabeth tore her eyes away from the waterfall. "Pretty far, I'd bet," she guessed. Her gaze fastened onto a few patches of light along the floor. "That's strange," she said, pointing them out to the others.

Randy scratched his chin, looking thoughtful.

"There must be little cracks in the ceiling that let light through." He squinted toward the top of the cave. "See? Right there—and there—and there."

Elizabeth followed his finger. Through little chinks she could clearly see the blue sky. "Neat," she said. "So if we have to go further back for some strange reason—" She tried hard to keep her voice as cheerful as possible. "Then we'll have light to see by. Right?"

"Right," Amy said, not sounding cheerful at all.

Maria cleared her throat. "Um—not that I'm worried or anything," she began, "but maybe we should move back a few steps. Just in case."

"Yeah," Randy chimed in. "It's better to have your back against the wall. Not that I'm scared. Just . . . in case."

Elizabeth nodded. "Just in case," she echoed, taking a couple of steps back—and then a few more. *Just in case.*

"Get your foot off my elbow, *please*," Lila said in a brittle voice.

"Well, if you would just keep your elbows to yourself—" Bruce snapped.

There's got to be more room in here, Jessica thought. It probably hadn't been more than five minutes since they'd tumbled into the pit, but it seemed like an hour. Jessica wished her friends would learn to stand still.

"The next person who kicks me, dies," Aaron announced.

Jessica's fingers groped for the back of the pit, but she couldn't find it. "Hey, guys." Her voice was low.

No point in letting wild animals hear us! "There's more room back here."

"Hurray," Lila said primly, stepping toward Jessica. "Now I can breathe again." She frowned. "Why is there light here?" she asked suspiciously. "Who brought a flashlight and didn't tell me?"

Bewildered, Jessica looked around. There *did* seem to be a few dim shafts of light piercing the cavern. *Hmm*—"It's the ceiling, Lila," she told her friend, pointing above her head. "See those little cracks? The sunshine comes through, just enough to see."

"At last you've done something right, Jessica," Janet said. "Move over and let me in where it's light."

"It's only barely light," Jessica told her.

"What about the light?" Janet cupped a hand to her ear. "Speak up."

"Only *barely*," Jessica said, afraid to speak much louder. Next to her, Aaron stiffened. "We should keep moving back," he said in an unusually high voice. "Just in case something tries to, you know, come through the entrance."

Barely—bear-ly. Jessica shivered. She knew what Aaron was thinking. "Aaron's right," she said. "It's better to keep our backs to the wall."

"Bruce will protect us," Janet said firmly. She shuffled backward. "Won't you, Bruce?"

Jessica was still clutching her stick. *Elizabeth would know what to do,* she thought, swallowing hard and wishing her sister were there. *She's always so thoughtful and so calm.* Step by step, stick in one hand, Jessica backed slowly away from the hole through which Mandy had fallen. With the other hand she groped for the rear wall of the cave.

In the underground silence Jessica found herself wondering if the cavern would go on forever. She edged around a rock, but the passage continued. When she finally touched a wall, it was only the side of the cave slowly bending around. The passage kept going. *It feels like we've been here at least three hours,* Jessica thought, running her hand along the wall. She wasn't sure she could still see the entrance to the cave. *We'd better come to the end soon.*

Carefully Jessica transferred her stick from her right hand to her left. Then she groped behind her with her right hand, reaching for the wall—reaching, reaching—

Her hand brushed against something unexpected. Jessica's heart stopped. Whatever it was felt warm.

Warm—and furry.

Dropping her stick, Jessica screamed.

Five

A pirate! Elizabeth thought as something in the darkness brushed against her sweatshirt. *Or a cannibal!* Her mouth opened and closed frantically. But no sound came out. *They're here,* she thought miserably. *And now they'll—*

An earsplitting scream tore through the cavern. *It sounds like it's right next to my head,* Elizabeth thought as it echoed and reechoed off the rocky walls. Whirling around in the dim light, she found herself staring right into—

A mirror.

That's me. Elizabeth gasped, stepping back. In front of her was her own image. She recognized her own face screwed up with terror, dirty and bruised—and—

Wait a minute! Elizabeth blinked again. *No, it couldn't be.* The long blond hair was completely dry, not wet and tangled like her own. Instinctively she reached up and patted her hair. *Still dripping. And the reflection didn't move its own hand, which means—*

"Jessica!" Elizabeth squealed with delight, throwing herself into her twin's arms.

By the time Elizabeth was done hugging her, Jessica was pretty wet. Not that she cared. "I can't believe you're safe," she gasped, the words tumbling over each other in her effort to get them out. "We were so scared! We thought there were animals, and then we heard screams, and then—"

"*You* thought there were animals," Janet said.

"Yeah, *you* thought there were animals," Bruce echoed.

"You thought there were animals?" Elizabeth stared at Jessica in surprise. "That's weird! We were certain there were people on the island."

"There were," Aaron said dryly. "Us."

"No, I mean—" Elizabeth clapped her hand over her mouth. "Oh, wow! I bet we were hearing you every time we thought we heard the pirates or whatever."

"The *pirates*?" Jessica repeated.

Elizabeth blushed. "Kind of silly, huh?"

Jessica's eyes danced. "Silly, all right. Of course, *we* thought we were hearing lions and bears when we were really only hearing *you*."

"So we're really the only ones on this island?" Mandy asked.

"Unless the hijackers made it," Jessica replied, snorting to show how much she thought of that idea.

"No way," Bruce said. He curled his lip. "We had them tied up. They're dead meat by now. Fish food."

"Shark bait," Aaron agreed with a laugh.

"Well, you don't have to sound so happy about it," Elizabeth murmured.

Jessica took a close look at her sister's face. "What do you mean, Lizzie?" she asked.

Elizabeth sighed. "Oh, I don't know. I guess I just feel a little guilty. Almost like we killed them or something."

"Oh, come *on*!" Bruce groaned. "Listen, it was them or us, right?" He stared down at Elizabeth. "And I don't know about you, but I'm just as happy it was us. You want to go take their place, be my guest."

"That isn't really what I meant," Elizabeth said sadly.

Jessica put an arm around her twin's shoulder. "I know what you mean," she said, giving Elizabeth a squeeze. "But, you know, it's a lot better than the alternative."

"What alternative?" Elizabeth looked blank.

"They could be here on the island with us," Jessica pointed out.

Elizabeth let out a deep breath. "I hear you," she said.

Jessica grinned. "Now let's get out of here and figure out what to do next."

"So this wasn't really a cave at all," Maria mused as the group headed toward the entrance by the waterfall.

"More like a tunnel," Elizabeth said with a nod. She turned to look behind her. "See, it bends halfway in the middle. You can't see the other entrance from here. You can't even tell it exists."

"Pretty neat," Mandy said admiringly. "It goes right under the hill, I guess."

They clambered through the passage and hiked down the rocky ledge. Elizabeth blinked as she came out into the bright sunshine. One by one the others followed.

"Now what?" Janet asked sourly as she emerged from between the rocks.

"No more climbing, *please,*" Lila put in. "I'm totally out of breath." She gave a few hurried wheezes as if to prove it.

"Climbing?" Elizabeth whispered to Amy. Her eyes twinkled.

Amy grinned back. "You call *that* climbing?"

Bruce cleared his throat. "Attention, please." He paused, and Elizabeth looked at him reluctantly. "We're going to have to stay alive on this island somehow. Since I've been a Boy Scout for a whole bunch of years, I know more about this stuff than you do. So you need to listen to me." His eyes traveled around the group. "And Janet, because she's an eighth-grader."

"And president of the Unicorns," Janet added proudly.

Elizabeth suppressed a shudder. Privately she and her friends called the Unicorns the Snob Squad.

"We'll have to build a fire," Bruce went on, "and get some food."

Maria nudged Elizabeth. "Bruce—" she began.

Bruce walked past Maria and sat down on the other side of the pool, facing the waterfall. "Fires aren't too hard to build, you know," he continued. "If you're a Boy Scout, like me. You guys should all be glad you've got an experienced pro here with you." He jerked his thumb toward his chest. "I mean me, of course."

"*And* an eighth-grader," Janet pointed out. "Who also happens to be the president of—"

"Right," Maria interrupted, following Bruce, "but—"

"Just listen to *Bruce,*" Janet said. "Bruce is the expert. Tell them, Lila."

"He's the expert, all right," Lila agreed, wincing as she walked around the rocks. "He told you so himself."

"Besides which, he saved my life," Janet went on. "Didn't you, Bruce?"

Maria scratched her head. "I'm sure he knows a lot, Janet. I just wanted to—"

"Obviously," Bruce broke in, "the first thing to do is sharpen some sticks and hunt some wild animals."

Sharpen sticks? Wild animals? Elizabeth stared at Bruce in confusion. "Um, Bruce," she ventured, "I thought we just agreed there weren't any wild animals here."

"Yeah." Maria put her hands on her hips. "Did you see any tracks?"

"And how are you planning to sharpen the sticks anyway?" Randy chimed in.

Bruce's shoulders twitched. He gave an exaggerated sigh. "Well, if you want to do without food," he said loudly, staring toward Janet and Lila as though to ask, *Aren't they being stupid?*

Maria shook her head. "There's plenty of melons," she argued. "We've been eating them all day. If you ask me, hunting is a waste of time."

"Well, who *did* ask you?" Lila folded her arms across her chest. "This is so boring, Bruce," she said, blinking rapidly. "If they don't want to come with *us*, then who needs them?"

Elizabeth cringed at the way she emphasized the word *us*.

"What's your suggestion?" Janet said, staring hard at Maria. "If you don't have a better plan, then you should just shut up. Don't you think so, Lila?"

"Oh, yes," Lila agreed.

Maria shrugged. "I don't know if I have a better plan or not," she said. Janet snorted. "But I do know that we should all help plan, instead of taking orders from Bruce—no matter how many times he's been camping."

Elizabeth nodded. "I think our biggest problem is how to get off this island," she said slowly. "I think we need to work on that before we make big plans about—"

Janet yawned.

"We need a big SOS," Maria said. "So if a plane flies over—"

"Who needs an SOS?" Bruce sounded annoyed. "I've got that covered already. We just set the woods on fire, and—"

Amy shuddered. "And burn ourselves to a cinder? Count me out!"

"Bruce knows how to set fires," Lila argued. "Good fires. The kind where you don't burn yourself up." She looked at Bruce. "Don't you, Bruce?"

"You bet," Bruce agreed. "What's your problem, Maria? You sound like you think I'm incompetent or something."

"I know!" Elizabeth jumped into the argument, aware that Maria was getting madder and madder. "Why don't we stamp a huge SOS into the sand? We can work together," she added quickly as a frown creased Janet's face. "It won't take long—"

"Bo-ring," Lila said.

"I mean, if we're going to be on a desert island, let's have some fun," Bruce argued. "An SOS in the sand, that's for wimps. Let's do it right."

"Like chopping down trees to spell out SOS in the forest?" Aaron suggested. He sat forward eagerly.

"Exactly." Bruce smiled with pleasure. "Now *that's* the kind of idea that makes sense. Let's have a few more of them, OK?"

"It's totally stupid." Maria fumed. She looked to her friends for help.

"What are you planning to use to cut the trees down?" Randy asked curiously.

Bruce waved his hand in the air. "Details," he explained. "Listen. The point is, we can worry about SOSes and shelter and stuff later. Right now we need to hunt."

"He's right, Maria," Lila agreed. "Some of us are hungry. *Some* of us don't want to live on nothing but melons."

Elizabeth looked nervously at the group around her. *This is no good,* she thought, a hollow feeling at the pit of her stomach. *The last thing we need is to bicker. If we're going to make it out of here, we've got to pull together.*

"Well, it would be helpful if *some* of us had brains a little bigger than a melon!" Maria snapped, frustrated. She turned to Elizabeth. "Come on, Elizabeth. Tell these jokers what we need to do."

"Yeah, Elizabeth," Amy urged her. "You always have good ideas."

Elizabeth gulped. *I don't know if I want to be a*

leader, a small voice inside her protested, but there seemed to be no choice.

"Well . . ." she began.

"That's stupid," Janet said loftily.

Elizabeth blushed. "No, it's not," she protested. "See, there are already rain clouds moving in from the sea."

She pointed, and Jessica followed her finger. *She's right,* Jessica thought with a twinge of concern. *Those sure look like rain clouds to me.* "But why does that mean we have to build a shelter right now?" she asked aloud. "Why can't we just sleep in the tunnel, like Bruce suggested?"

Elizabeth curled her lip. "Do you really want to spend the night there, Jess? We don't know what might be inside. Maybe spiders."

Jessica bit her lip while she thought about this. *How afraid of spiders am I really?* "But it would be more fun to sleep in the tunnel," she argued. "More like roughing it." *Not that afraid,* she decided.

Anyway, building a shelter would be a lot of work.

Bruce made a sound deep in his throat. "She's right, Elizabeth," he said. "You should listen to your sister for a change. Jessica's got some great ideas."

Jessica's heart jumped. *So what if Bruce is usually kind of obnoxious?* she thought. *It's not every day I get a compliment from the cutest guy at school!* "And besides," she went on, a little more boldly, "you keep saying we shouldn't leave this waterfall, and I don't understand why not."

"It's already giving me a headache," Janet muttered, covering her ears. "Does anybody have an aspirin?"

Elizabeth took a deep breath. "Because as far as we know, this is the only source of fresh water on the island."

Bruce smirked. "As far as we *know,*" he pointed out. "As far as we *know,* there might be a big lake on the other side of the hill."

"There probably is," Jessica agreed, speaking to her sister but staring right at Bruce. "Bruce sounds like he knows what he's talking about."

"Jessica!" Elizabeth put her hands on her hips in dismay.

"Well, he does!" Jessica felt a little guilty about abandoning her sister—but just a little. "I'm sorry, but he does!" She rubbed her cheek. "Listen, Lizzie, this could be an incredibly awesome adventure. But your ideas just don't sound like they'd be much fun."

"Maybe not." Elizabeth folded her arms. "But, Jess, we have to be safe. Don't you see? I mean—"

"I know, I know!" Jessica grimaced. *Why can't Elizabeth come up with ideas that are sensible—and fun, too?* "I just think—" She hesitated, torn between loyalty to her friends and loyalty to her sister.

"Hey, Jessica," Bruce said, his voice smooth as velvet. "Did anyone ever tell you that your eyes are exactly the color of the ocean here?"

Jessica swung around to look at Bruce. He grinned at her and winked.

Well, obnoxious as he was, it was a surprisingly easy decision when you came right down to it. "Whatever you say, Bruce," she said, not looking at her sister.

* * *

That evening the group dined on melons and two extremely bony fish that had washed up on the beach. Elizabeth chewed her meal in silence, replaying the day in her mind.

Most of it was pretty forgettable.

How should you make a campfire? she thought. *Ask Bruce, the Boy Scout. Ha!* Bruce hadn't been able to get one going. He'd blamed it on the wind. *Yeah, right.* In the end, Amy and Maria had managed to get a few sticks to light.

Then there was the tiny thatched roof that Elizabeth and her friends had made while Bruce and *his* buddies—*including Jessica,* Elizabeth thought with a pang—had walked up and down the hill with their sort-of sharp sticks. Elizabeth glanced up at the cloudy sky. *Well, if it rains,* she thought, forcing a laugh, *there might be room for four of us under there. Five, if they're small.*

And then there was—

Elizabeth sighed and thought about what there *wasn't.* No SOS, anywhere. No food but melons and the two bony fish. No way of getting off the island.

And no teamwork.

She huddled closer to the fire. *Amy, Maria, Todd, Cammi,* she thought to herself, her eyes traveling in a circle. Next came a big blank spot. Her eyes leaped over to Lila. *Lila, Jessica, Aaron, Bruce . . . Honestly! Can't we even sit together?*

"Pass the water, please." Elizabeth nudged Amy.

"Oh, it's gone," Amy replied, holding out a seashell they'd been drinking from. "Want me to fill it again?" She rose from her seat.

Across the circle Elizabeth saw Janet take a drink

from another shell. *There's plenty in that one,* she thought. *I could just ask Janet to pass it over here, and then Amy wouldn't have to get up.*

Across the campfire, Janet giggled and laid her head on Bruce's shoulder. "Oh, Bruce," she cooed, "you're so *funny*!"

Elizabeth wrinkled her nose in disgust. Sighing, she got up and reached for Amy's seashell. "Thanks, anyway," she said. "But I'll fill it myself."

Six

"These melons are getting old fast," Mandy muttered the next morning, gnawing her way down to a green rind. "We've only been on this island for a day, and I feel like I've already eaten six gazillion of them."

"I know what you mean," Jessica agreed. Every bone in her body ached from last night. The sand hadn't been as soft as it had appeared, and she'd gotten much less sleep than she'd wanted. "Whatever happened to bacon and eggs, anyway?"

"Pancakes." Lila sighed dreamily.

"French toast dripping with maple syrup," Aaron said, licking his lips.

"Oh, come on," Elizabeth said from a few feet away. "They're not that bad." She took a big bite of her own piece. "See?"

"Yuck," Jessica said, drawing back in disgust. "You're not telling me you actually like those melons! Don't you have any taste buds?" She dropped the remains of her own melon on the ground. "If we ever get off this island, I'm never eating fresh fruit again."

"So what are we doing today, anyway?" Mandy asked, dropping her own melon. "I don't feel very hungry any more."

"Well," Elizabeth began, "I think we should split up and explore the island, see if there's more fresh water—things like that."

"You would think so," Janet said, rolling her eyes.

"Makes sense to me," Maria said.

Me too, Jessica thought. But first she stole a look at Bruce.

"I'm going to stay here, thanks," he said importantly from his spot opposite the waterfall.

Elizabeth frowned. "How come?"

"Bruce has a very good reason," Janet said quickly. She stared hard at Jessica.

"Oh, he does," Jessica agreed, even though she had no clue what Janet was talking about. "A *very* good reason. We talked about it last night."

Elizabeth shrugged. "All right. We'll be back in a while, then." She stood up to go. Amy, Todd, and a few others followed her.

"Take your time," Jessica couldn't help shouting as they disappeared into the forest. Once they were gone, she turned to Bruce.

"OK, what's the plan?" she asked impatiently.

"I wish those guys would work *with* us," Maria said as she and Elizabeth walked onto the beach at the other side of the island. Their group had split into two to explore, agreeing to meet back at the waterfall when they were done.

"I know what you mean," Elizabeth responded. "And I hate to admit it, but Jessica's one of the worst." A flash of brown at the edge of the water caught her eye. "What's that?"

Maria followed her gaze. "I don't know."

Elizabeth sprinted forward, her feet slightly sinking into the sand. "It's a briefcase," she said with amazement, holding it up for Maria to see.

"A briefcase!" Maria exclaimed. "Then we must be near a town. Maybe we'll be rescued!"

"Wait a minute." Elizabeth shaded her eyes against the sun and stared down the beach. *What's that bobbing in the waves over there?* Taking off her shoes, she waded into the surf. "I think there's another one, too."

"Can you reach it?" Maria asked.

"I think so." This beach was rockier than the other, and Elizabeth nearly lost her balance once or twice. *Another couple of steps . . .* Leaning forward, Elizabeth plucked the other briefcase from a rock where it had been caught and waded ashore.

"You've got some seaweed on you," Maria said, stooping to pull it off Elizabeth's leg. "Yuck. I think I like the other side of the island better."

"Me too," Elizabeth agreed, examining the briefcases in front of her. They were worn and scuffed, and they looked identical. "I think they're part of a set."

"What's inside?" Maria asked.

"I guess we could open them," Elizabeth said doubtfully, her fingers reaching for the catch on the one nearest to her. "My dad's briefcase opens right about—here—ah." With a spring, the lid flew open. Elizabeth's face froze.

She drew back and swallowed hard. *It couldn't be,* she thought grimly. *It just couldn't be.*

"Will these do?" Mandy asked, dropping an armload of logs on the ground.

Bruce frowned down at her. "This one's too short," he said, plucking a stick out of the pile and tossing it into the pool. "And these are too crooked. The others are OK. I guess."

"Well, maybe if you'd help us look, too," Jessica suggested. She stood behind Mandy, her arms full of vines she'd gathered from the forest. Beside her Aaron nodded in agreement.

"Don't be silly, Jessica," Janet said. She stood next to Bruce, her arms folded firmly across her chest. "If you'd spend more time getting what we need and less time criticizing our leader, we'd all be a lot better off. He *is* a Boy Scout, you know."

"I know!" Jessica said quickly. She knew what was coming next: *"And I'm an eighth-grader,"* she mimicked Janet in her mind.

"And I'm an eighth-grader," Janet said primly.

Jessica sighed. Like a Unicorn who knew what was good for her, she wanted to please Janet, but she had to admit, her friend's bossiness was starting to get on her nerves. And it wasn't much fun to obey Bruce's orders either, especially since he hadn't paid her any compliments in quite a while. "Are these vines OK with you?" Jessica asked, dumping them next to Janet. She wanted to add "Your Highness," but she thought she'd better not.

"Hmm . . ." Janet squinted at the pile. "What do you think, Bruce?"

Before he could answer, Maria and Elizabeth ran up to them. They were breathing hard, their faces red, their eyes open wide. The rest of their friends followed them, looking frantic.

"Elizabeth, what's going on?" Jessica asked anxiously.

"You'll never guess what we've found!" Elizabeth gasped, her chest heaving.

Maria thrust a briefcase on the ground. "Feast your eyes!"

Jessica frowned. "A briefcase? That's what you're so excited about? It's not even as nice as Dad's."

"Open it!" Elizabeth's voice was insistent.

Shrugging, Jessica knelt down. *Elizabeth and her friends sometimes get excited over the silliest things,* she thought as she started to unfasten the latch. *Homework and books and briefcases and—* She blinked down at the briefcase in front of her. "It's—it's money."

"Money?" Janet repeated. "Let me see!" She and Bruce pushed their way forward to look.

Jessica blinked again. It was money all right, pile upon pile of crisp green bills. "But who carries money around in briefcases?" she asked, reaching out to touch the waterproof plastic bag in which the bills were wrapped. Her fingers recoiled. "Elizabeth, they're—they're—*hundred-dollar* bills!"

"No way!" Bruce stared over Jessica's shoulder.

Jessica smoothed the plastic and showed him. *I don't think I've ever seen one of these before,* she thought, feeling slightly faint.

"There's got to be ten thousand bucks in here." Bruce stared in disbelief.

"More than that," Elizabeth said, standing opposite Jessica. "Say two hundred bills in each stack—two cases—" She bit her lip. "It's in the millions. Four or five million dollars."

Jessica felt her throat catch. *Five million dollars!*

"You know what this is, don't you?" Elizabeth asked.

Jessica nodded. "It must be from the ferryboat," she responded, dropping her voice almost to a whisper. She didn't dare say the rest out loud:

It's what the robbers stole from the bank before they hijacked our boat!

"OK, we've got to do something with this money," Bruce said authoritatively a few moments later. "Got it! We'll put it over in that tunnel we found yesterday."

"It doesn't really matter where we put it," Jessica murmured. "I mean, there's nobody else around. Who's going to take the money?" She forced a laugh, but no one joined her. "And it doesn't even belong to us, anyway."

"Right." Amy sounded nervous.

I can't believe this, Jessica told herself. She took another look at the pile of money. *All my life I've dreamed of having a million bucks. Now it's sitting right here, and I don't even want to touch it!* She picked at the plastic bag in front of her. *It's almost as though I'm afraid that the hijackers will show up if I do—*

Which is crazy. Of course.

Jessica licked her lips nervously. "Well, we might

as well, um, put the money in the tunnel just—just because. There was a rock near where Mandy fell in," she offered. "On that side of the tunnel. I'll go in the waterfall entrance and hide it."

"I'll go, too," Elizabeth said.

"Two Wakefields with five million dollars?" Bruce exclaimed. "Not on your life! I'm coming, too!"

"Just what do you think we're going to do with the money—rent a helicopter?" Elizabeth asked.

"What about me?" Janet asked before he could respond. She smiled up at Bruce. "You're not planning to leave me here with all these other people—are you?"

"We need you to stay here and be in charge while Bruce is gone," Jessica answered quickly. "We need someone who knows what she's doing. Someone who's an eighth-grader. You know. Just in case anything happens."

Janet tossed her head. "All right," she agreed, a smile creeping across her face. "Now, Aaron, about those vines—"

She was still talking when Jessica and the others disappeared behind the waterfall.

"So what have you been doing all morning, anyway?" Crouching in the tunnel, Elizabeth positioned the briefcases carefully behind the rock. *I hope this hiding place works!* she thought.

Bruce snickered and threw a handful of dirt on the briefcases. "While you've been waiting to be rescued," he said proudly, "we've been doing something about it."

Elizabeth raised her eyebrows. "You have?"

Bruce turned and led the way back toward the

waterfall. "We're building a raft. Then we'll sail away to freedom. You want to help, or are you planning to stay here till next July?"

A raft? Elizabeth looked questioningly at Maria. "Do you think we can build a raft solid enough to—"

"Do I think so? I *know* so," Bruce said proudly as the group returned to where Janet and the others were standing. He gestured toward the pieces of wood and vine that lay at his feet.

Janet brushed some hair off her forehead. "You have to remember, Elizabeth, Bruce is—"

"A Boy Scout," Elizabeth finished for her. She looked down at the pile of mismatched logs and sticks. *Do they give merit badges for raft building?* she wondered.

"And *I'm* an eighth-grader," Janet reminded her.

"As though being an eighth-grader has anything to do with anything," Elizabeth whispered to Maria as Jessica, Bruce, and Janet walked ahead of them.

Maria grinned. "What do you think?" she asked. "Should we help out?"

"I guess it can't hurt," Elizabeth said doubtfully.

Maria nodded. "I don't think they can finish a raft all by themselves, but maybe if we all pitch in, it'll work."

Elizabeth smiled, feeling a twinge of hope. "Maybe we can all work together for once."

"Why do we need all that mud?" Lila demanded, wrinkling her nose.

Amy forced a smile. "We have to chink the cracks between the logs somehow, Lila."

"Not with mud we don't," Lila said, staring at the

mud that covered Amy's hand. She shuddered. "I mean, like, totally gross."

Amy took a deep breath. "What did you have in mind?"

"How about leaves?" Lila said vaguely. "Anything but *mud*. I don't want to get my hands dirty."

Amy clenched and unclenched her muddy fists. Building a raft was turning out to be a lot harder than she had expected.

At the edge of the beach, Elizabeth wiped her sweaty forehead. "Shouldn't we be building this in the shade?" she asked wearily, letting her feet trail in the salty water. *The last thing I need right now is a sunburn.*

Bruce sighed impatiently. "The point of a raft, Elizabeth," he said, as though talking to a five-year-old, "is to sail it in the ocean. The ocean," he continued before Elizabeth could speak, "is *here*. The shade is *there*." He stared at her scornfully.

"We could carry it down—" Elizabeth began.

"Why don't we just carry the shade down here while we're at it?" Bruce snarled. He shook his head and reached for another vine. "Got any more bright ideas?"

"What do you mean, we need more space? What on earth are you talking about?" Jessica asked, her eyes flashing. She stared at the frame that Cammi and Mandy were building. "We're going to have *plenty* of room."

"No, we're not," Maria protested. "Think about it. Say we each sit in a rectangle that's a foot on one side and two feet on the other—"

"You'd have to be pretty fat to need that much room," Jessica replied hotly. *Honestly,* she thought, *why won't Maria listen to me?* She tried again. "This is about a foot, right?" she asked, holding her hands apart. "Then—"

"No way!" Maria stared at her. "*This* is a foot!" She held her hands a few inches closer together than Jessica's.

"Uh-uh!" Jessica couldn't believe her eyes. "My brother told me once that it takes a stack of twenty-four CD boxes to make a foot." *Or did he say thirty-six?* "You've got, like, thirteen CD boxes. Maybe only ten. Twenty-four is *this* much." She spread her hands again, a little wider than before.

"CD boxes? What in the world are you talking about?" Maria said.

Jessica let out an exasperated sigh. "Oh, please. If I have to explain *that* to you, we're in serious trouble." Breathing deeply, she turned her back and walked away.

"It's all your fault it's taken us this long," Bruce said accusingly, pulling the last vine tight. He shook his head. "I mean, all day building a lousy raft."

"I'm sorry," Elizabeth replied exhaustedly. She looked at the sky. They had worked on the raft for what felt like forever. Soon it would be dark. "But you weren't exactly cooperative yourself, you know."

"Who decided to build half the raft all by themselves?" Bruce jeered. "Up by the trees, where they could protect their beautiful skin from the big bad sun?"

"Who decided they could only use logs found by their friends?" Amy jumped in.

Elizabeth took a deep breath. "Look, it's finished," she said, trying to be reasonable. "That's what counts. And we'll try it first thing in the morning, all right?"

"If it hadn't been for you," Lila said bitingly, "we'd be home by now."

"If it hadn't been for *us*," Todd shot back, "you'd have sunk out there, first thing. This way you've got a *real* raft."

"Yeah, right." Janet rolled her eyes.

Elizabeth looked at the raft. It was a sorry sight. The two halves had been lashed together at last, but they were different sizes and curved apart alarmingly. Some chinks were filled with mud, others were stuffed with leaves. "Tomorrow," she said as firmly as she could. "Tomorrow we'll try it out. Right now we'll have some dinner." *There,* she thought. *That ought to calm them down.*

"Dinner of what?" Lila asked suspiciously.

Elizabeth shrugged. "Melons, I guess."

"Yeah?" Bruce jumped up and looked at Elizabeth accusingly. "And you know whose fault *that* is—"

Elizabeth stifled a groan. It was going to be a long evening.

Later that night Jessica awoke and sat bolt upright. She'd had a weird dream, she realized—a dream about two shadowy figures prowling around near the campfire.

Hmm, she thought, staring off over the dark sea.

The only lights came from the stars, along with a flickering glow from what remained of the campfire. Even so, the dream seemed unusually vivid. Jessica cocked her head and listened. But all she heard was the gentle roar of the waterfall and the familiar lapping of waves against the beach.

Just in case, Jessica walked over to the raft and looked at the ground around it. *Plenty of footprints here,* she thought. *Of course,* she reminded herself, *we've been walking around the beach all day.* She stooped and tried to measure the footprints by hand. A couple did look bigger than the rest, but it was hard to tell.

Jessica yawned. She looked down at her sleeping sister, curled up next to Amy. "Must have been Todd," she murmured. "Or maybe Randy." She yawned again. *Maybe they just couldn't sleep. It happens.* The dream seemed less real to her now than it had a few minutes ago.

Feeling tired, Jessica went back to her place on the beach and curled up next to Lila. *I'll ask them in the morning,* she promised herself just before she drifted into sleep once again.

Seven

"It's a beautiful day to go sailing . . ." Elizabeth sang happily to herself as she ate the last of her melon bright and early the next morning. She had to admit, Jessica was right—melons got awfully tiresome after a while. She'd be glad when she could eat something else.

"Everybody ready?" Bruce asked, springing to his feet and staring out to sea. "The wind won't keep blowing forever, you know. The sooner we get going—"

"Me first!" Lila sprinted down toward the raft. "I have a hairdresser appointment this afternoon," she explained, crawling out to the farthest corner, "and she really hates to be kept waiting."

"Glad we could help," Amy whispered in Elizabeth's ear.

Elizabeth grinned. The raft still looked pretty rickety, but she had a surge of hope. *Yup, I think we can do it!*

"We should bring a few melons," Maria suggested as the other kids piled on.

Bruce stared at her. "Why in the world would we want to do something like that?" he said. Janet stuck out her tongue and pretended to gag.

"Just in case," Maria explained. "I mean, if it's farther than we think, or if the wind stops, or—" She shrugged.

"To be safe," Elizabeth added.

"Safe, schmafe," Bruce muttered. "All right. No harm in it, I guess." He clambered aboard the raft. "OK! Hit me with a bomb!" he yelled to Todd.

Todd grinned and picked up a big ripe melon. "Fire one!" he called, lobbing it through the air. It spun lazily to Bruce's left. "Too far!" Bruce yelled, leaping sideways across Lila.

"Watch it!" Lila screeched, grabbing the edge of the raft.

Splash! Elizabeth shut her eyes instinctively as Bruce caught the melon—and, in the next moment, plummeted into the ocean. An instant later he surfaced, grinning and holding the melon aloft like a football. "Touchdown!" he yelled happily.

"Yes!" Todd thrust both arms in the air. "Hey, Elizabeth, want to see it again in slow motion?" He picked up another melon. Taking exaggerated steps, he moved back and raised his arm jerkily. Elizabeth laughed.

"Time!" Bruce called. He swam to the raft and hopped on. "OK, now!"

As the second melon flew through the air, Elizabeth leaped up and caught it with one hand. "Interception!" she yelled, prancing through the waves.

"Hey!" Bruce shouted with a laugh.

That's a switch! Elizabeth thought at the sound of his laughter. She passed the melon to Bruce, who plunked it down on the raft. *At least we're all having fun together,* she thought happily.

For a change!

"Good-bye, island!" Jessica shouted a few minutes later. She breathed in the salty air as Bruce and Todd shoved off and the raft began to glide through the water. "Now, *this* is the life."

"The only way to travel," Mandy agreed.

"It would be," Janet said sourly, "if Cammi would stop hogging all the room."

"Me?" Cammi asked, hugging her knees tightly. "I have hardly any room at all. Ask Mandy to move over. She's the one who's taking up all the space."

"I am not!" Mandy said. "I have, like, maybe two inches."

There was a splash as Todd and Bruce jumped aboard. "Hold still!" Jessica commanded as the raft began to rock. She pushed down with her palms against the logs. *Uh-oh.* One of them seemed to be moving more than the others.

"Move *over,*" Janet hissed.

"I'm trying!" *Was that Cammi?* Jessica wondered, not daring to turn around. There was a sudden movement, and her end of the raft dipped way down. "Watch it!" she cried angrily as waves covered her knees.

"I'm getting wet!" someone screamed. *Lila.*

"You're going to be a lot wetter if you don't sit down and shut up!" *That sounded like Todd,* Jessica thought, trying to swivel around to see without losing her balance.

"Why don't we all trail our feet in the water like Amy?" Elizabeth asked. "That might save a little space."

"And have sharks nibble our toes? No, thanks!" Janet replied. Amy gave a little shriek and jerked her legs up. Once again Jessica felt the raft drop out from under her.

"Um—if you don't mind," Bruce said sarcastically, "some of us would like to sit down? Before we fall overboard?" Jessica could see him trying to wedge his way between Todd and Mandy.

"And if *you* don't mind," Todd shot back, "*some* of us would like to make it back to Sweet Valley? Without being stepped on?"

The raft had swung around in the current, and Jessica now faced the island. They didn't seem to have gotten very far. "Can everybody just hold still?" Elizabeth asked.

Jessica snorted. "*Some* of us feel like we're about to be washed overboard."

"Oh, yeah? Who was the one who said we didn't need this much room?" Maria asked, gritting her teeth.

"We have plenty of space!" Jessica said angrily, feeling someone's arm pressing into her back. She jiggled an arm without touching anybody else. "See?"

"If I have to sit like this all the way to California, my knees will go to sleep," Janet said in a dark voice. "Permanently."

"Tough noogies," Amy said.

"Please, you guys!" Elizabeth yelled just as Aaron gasped.

"Water's coming through the cracks!" he shouted.

Alarmed, Jessica glanced down. The leaves she and her friends had so carefully stuffed into the cracks were falling to pieces in the cool water. "Plug the holes!" she shouted, frantically trying to stick her finger in an empty space.

"Too late for that!" Maria called. "The vines are coming loose!"

Sure enough, Jessica felt a sudden lurch. One of the logs she was sitting on headed south while the one next to it went north.

"We're doomed!" Amy yelled.

"Real helpful, Amy," Jessica said, trying to pull the logs back together with her free hand. *No good.*

"Abandon ship!" Bruce commanded.

Jessica's heart pounded as she jumped quickly over what remained of the side of the raft. All around her there were splashes.

"Swim for it!" Jessica called out. She set off with sure, swift strokes toward the sandy beach.

"Elizabeth? Shouldn't we get off the raft and swim for it?" Todd asked.

Elizabeth looked at the pieces of the raft that remained. The part she was sitting on was only three logs wide. Water bubbled between the cracks. "I guess so," she said sadly. She and Todd were the only ones left on the raft. "I was really hoping this would work."

"I know." Todd shook his head.

Elizabeth took a deep breath. "All right. When I say three, we'll jump for it. One . . . two . . ."

"Look out, Elizabeth!"

As Elizabeth opened her mouth to say *three*, the logs slipped out from under her feet, and she slowly sank down into the green-blue sea. Out of the corner of her eye she saw a wave approaching, scarcely any faster than a snail, and on the crest of the wave there was something that looked familiar—*two logs*, she thought, *fastened together by a piece of broken vine*—and then the logs began coming down, down, down, down, down, faster and faster even in slow motion, and at the last possible second, Elizabeth tried to twist her body so they wouldn't crash on top of her skull—

And then there was an ominous thud.

Feeling suddenly light-headed, Elizabeth reached out toward the sun. In the distance she could hear someone yell "Elizabeth!" *I wonder what they want*, Elizabeth thought. Feeling oddly exhausted, she opened her mouth to yawn. *That's strange.* Her mouth filled with water.

I should spit this out, Elizabeth told herself, but there didn't seem to be anywhere to spit it. She spun around, shutting her eyes as she did so. *I'm so tired* —

A hand reached down and seized her roughly by the arm. "Hey!" Elizabeth tried to shout, but no sound came out. She tried to shake off the intruder, but she felt herself being pulled up, up, up—and suddenly there was light and brightness all around. To her dismay, Elizabeth found herself choking. She tasted salt.

"Yuck!" Elizabeth swallowed a mouthful of seawater. She realized that Todd's arms were around her. "Where am I?" She coughed.

"In the middle of the Pacific Ocean," Todd answered. "You hit your head. Are you all right?"

Elizabeth felt her body being leveled off. She

floated on her back, waves lapping around her ears. "No," she croaked. "I feel—sick."

"Okay. Just hold on." Todd kicked gracefully through the water. Elizabeth could feel his hands supporting her shoulders and the warm sun caressing her face. *That was a close call,* she realized.

And it was at that very moment that she blacked out.

The next thing Elizabeth knew, she was lying on the beach, her friends gathered close around her.

"She's awake." Maria was looking down at her. "Are you all right, Elizabeth?"

Elizabeth managed a croak.

"How many fingers am I holding up?" Todd asked. Her eyes weren't quite focusing, but . . . the image waved and took shape. "Three. Four. No, three," she said a little more firmly.

"She's OK." Todd stepped aside as Elizabeth struggled to sit up.

Amy sighed with relief. "You're a hero, Todd."

"Well." Todd shrugged modestly.

"Of course you are," Cammi said. "I mean, the rest of us were practically at the beach already. If you hadn't caught her—"

Janet's voice cut through Cammi's like a knife. "*Some* people," she announced to Lila icily, "will do absolutely *anything* to get attention." She shot a glance at Elizabeth.

Huh? Elizabeth could only stare.

"Don't I know it," Lila said. "Of course"—she fixed Todd with a look—"I'd pick someone a little stronger to save me."

"There's only one person on this island who *really* saved someone's life," Janet went on, staring meaningfully at Bruce.

But Bruce was gazing out to sea, where Elizabeth could just make out the last little bits of raft drifting over the horizon. "We should still be out there," he muttered under his breath. "We should!" He shook his head. "There's only one thing that could have gone wrong."

"Yeah. We should have tied the ropes tighter," Randy remarked.

Bruce aimed a murderous look at Randy. "The *ropes* have nothing to do with it."

"No?" Randy asked meekly.

Bruce looked around the group, a gleam in his eye. "It was sabotaged."

"*What?*" Maria asked.

Elizabeth put her hand to her forehead. What was he talking about?

"*Someone* didn't want my idea to work," Bruce said accusingly. "*Someone* wanted the raft to fall apart. *Someone* untied the knots while we were sleeping." He pointed at Elizabeth. "It was *you,*" he spat out. "Admit it!"

"What? I—" Forgetting her head injury, Elizabeth stood up straight. "I didn't go anywhere near the raft last night!" she sputtered angrily. "Why in the world would I want it to break?" *How can you say such a terrible thing?* she wondered, looking to her friends for help. "Do you think I want to stay here for the rest of my life?"

Lila stared menacingly at Elizabeth. "Power, Elizabeth," she said. "That's what it's all about for you. Don't try to pretend."

"Really," Janet said, nodding in agreement. "You think we don't know how jealous you are of Bruce and his great ideas?"

Elizabeth gasped. "Jealous? But—but—" She couldn't get the words out.

"Are you out of your mind?" Amy stepped forward. "Elizabeth was the last person to leave that raft. Why would she sabotage it and then stay on it?"

Bruce sneered. "Staying on the raft was a perfect way to destroy the evidence."

"What evidence?" Todd snapped. "Anyway, it was your side of the boat that came apart first."

"It was those old leaves," Maria said. "They couldn't keep the water out."

"Besides, there wasn't enough room for all of us," Elizabeth added as calmly as she could, though her heart was beating rapidly. "It would have sunk anyway."

But Bruce and his friends continued to glare at her.

Jessica felt her face heat up as Bruce, Janet, and Lila flailed accusations at Elizabeth. She opened her mouth to defend her, but she was too shaken to speak.

After a moment, Mandy spoke up. "Elizabeth's right." She played with a lock of her hair. "I mean, the leaves didn't work the way we expected—"

"You stay out of it!" Janet snapped. "Don't you understand what Bruce is telling you?"

"Um—" Mandy began, looking at the ground.

"That girl over there," Bruce said firmly, "sabotaged *our* raft." He pointed at Elizabeth again. "Are you going to listen to her or to me?"

Mandy cast an anxious look at Janet, who was

staring at her threateningly. "Well, you, I guess."

"Darn right," Bruce said. He put his hands on his hips and stared at the kids in front of him. "Dallas? Whose side are you on?"

Jessica stole a quick glance at Aaron, who looked a little frightened. "Yours," he said weakly.

Jessica bit her lip, dreading what was coming next.

"Good." Bruce's gaze shifted to her. "Wakefield?"

Janet stared at her, folding her arms.

Jessica opened her mouth, then shut it. She didn't want to abandon her sister, but Janet looked very—demanding. And something was nagging at her memory—something about last night.

"Well?" Janet leaned forward, her eyes cold as ice.

"Um—" *What was it?* Jessica wondered, reaching back in her memory. *What was it about last night?* Suddenly, Jessica widened her eyes as it all came back to her. "The footprints!" She cried.

"What?" Elizabeth looked at her in confusion.

"I thought I heard someone skulking around the raft last night." The words came out in a rush, before Jessica realized what she was saying.

"Hmm." Bruce nodded with satisfaction. "So there's proof." He grinned at Jessica. "Good work, Wakefield!"

"Proof!" Elizabeth exclaimed. "What kind of proof is that?" She looked at Jessica pleadingly.

"You heard her, Elizabeth," Janet said quickly. "She heard someone on the beach last night." She smiled approvingly at Jessica. "Thank you, Jessica, for your honesty."

"Well, hey, you can always count on me," Jessica replied, blushing at Janet's praise.

"Oh, Jessica, not you, too!" Elizabeth bit her lip.

Jessica avoided her sister's eyes. *Well, it could have been Elizabeth, all right. I mean, she could have just been pretending to be asleep.* Besides, it was nice having Janet's approval.

"Well, it looks like we're all in agreement," Bruce said firmly. "So let's—"

A sudden buzzing noise interrupted him. Looking up, Jessica saw a plane flying low in the sky. "Oh—" She gasped, raising her arms to signal. But it was too late. In despair she watched as the plane disappeared over the horizon.

Jessica felt her heart drop.

"Great," Bruce said bitterly. "Just great."

Janet glared at Elizabeth. "You and your big ideas, Elizabeth," she snarled. "If you'd listened to Bruce, we'd have an SOS and the pilot would be rescuing us right now."

"And I'd be on time for the hairdresser," Lila pouted.

"You should talk!" Amy yelled. "Elizabeth has more sense in her pinky than any three of you put together!"

"This was a stupid place to be, anyway," Bruce said, staring contemptuously at the waterfall. "I'm out of here. Who's coming with me?"

"Me," Aaron seconded.

"Let's go, Jessica," Janet said as she and the other Unicorns followed him, too.

Out of the corner of her eye, Jessica could feel Elizabeth looking at her pleadingly, but she was too frustrated to care. It was easier just to follow Janet.

On her way down the beach, Jessica thought about looking back at her sister. But she didn't.

"I don't believe this," Elizabeth said brokenly, sinking down into the sand. She blinked back tears. "My own sister—" Stunned, she watched the others disappear from sight.

"Well, good riddance," Maria said at last.

"Yeah, who needs them?" Todd echoed her.

But Elizabeth said nothing. The pain in her head had been replaced by a gnawing feeling in the pit of her stomach. Her friends might be happy that the others had left, but Jessica's betrayal just made her miserable.

And things are only going to get worse before they get better, she predicted grimly.

Eight

"I could have sworn I put all the fruit on this rock last night," Mandy said early the next morning. She twisted her fingers together nervously. "I mean, it couldn't have gotten up all by itself and just walked away."

Jessica frowned. "Are you positive you didn't move it someplace else, Mandy?" she asked. *Fruit for breakfast is bad enough,* she thought with distaste, thinking of the last three—or was it four?—meals she'd eaten. *But no breakfast at all—*

She grimaced. No breakfast at all sounded ten times worse.

"See, if you'd all come hunting last night with Aaron and me—" Bruce began.

"What did you guys catch besides a few mosquito bites?" Mandy asked sarcastically. "If we'd all gone hunting last night, we'd have nothing at all."

Bruce rolled his eyes. "What do we have now?" he demanded. "Nothing!"

Jessica had to admit, he was right. She tried to ignore the hunger pangs in her stomach. "But it doesn't make sense," she argued. "I distinctly remember collecting fruit yesterday before sunset. Janet, you were there, and Mandy, and—" Her eyes lit upon Lila. "Well, not Lila, I guess." *"There might be bugs on the fruit!"* She could hear Lila's voice echoing in her mind. *"Yecch! Count me out!"*

"And I put them right here on the rock," Mandy went on, "and where are they now?" She looked around, a frown on her face. "It's not like there are tons of other places where they could be."

Jessica surveyed their surroundings. They had camped near the headwaters of the stream, where there was plenty of fresh water. The area was open and grassy, with rocks and trees scattered here and there. She scratched her nose thoughtfully. *Guess I got a little too much sun yesterday.*

"Animals?" Aaron looked hopeful. "Elephants, maybe, or wild horses?" He grabbed his stick eagerly. "Hey, Bruce, let's—"

"Wild horses?" Lila squealed indignantly. She reached over and grabbed the sort-of sharp end of Aaron's stick. "Wild horses are beautiful creatures, and you have no right to destroy them."

"They're endangered, too," Mandy pointed out.

"Lila's right." Janet glared balefully at Aaron. "Wild horses are an important part of nature. As soon as we get back to Sweet Valley, the Unicorn Club will have a massive fund-raiser to help save the wild horses. Jessica?" Her voice was firm. "Don't you think that's a good idea?"

"Uh-huh," Jessica agreed. "Only a total dweeb

would want to kill a wild horse." In her mind's eye she saw a herd of wild horses galloping across the grass, their long manes flowing in the wind, their beautiful tawny skin glistening in the sunlight. She could see it all now. *Aaron would be rising up with his spear to kill the leader of the pack,* Jessica told herself, *but I would grab his weapon at the last minute and thrust my own body in the way.* She saw herself telling Aaron to kill her instead of the horse, if he had to be so bloodthirsty. *Then tears would come to Aaron's eyes, and he would come to his senses and beg for my forgiveness. And he'd throw away his weapon and vow never to kill another beautiful wild creature.*

"Hey, yeah, we could have a party to save the horses," Lila said happily.

"And circulate petitions," Mandy added, her eyes brightening.

"All right, all right!" Aaron burst out. Jessica found herself a little disappointed that he was convinced so easily. "How about a bear, then? That OK with you?"

Jessica looked at Mandy, who looked at Lila, who looked at Janet. "OK with me," Janet said with a shrug.

Really, Jessica thought. *I mean, who could get excited about bears?*

"Check." Aaron hefted his stick in the air and glanced over to Bruce. "Coming, Bruce?" he asked. "Bruce?"

Jessica glanced at Bruce, who was staring into the distance, a sharp frown on his face.

"Bruce?" Aaron raised his voice.

"It's got to be Elizabeth again," Bruce muttered. He balled his hands into fists.

"What are you talking about?" Jessica asked.

"While you guys were babbling about horses, I've been doing some thinking," Bruce snapped. "Who else would have stolen all our fruit? Who else would leave us here to starve?" He dropped his voice to a low whisper. "I'll tell you who. The same know-it-all who sabotaged the raft and made sure the airplane didn't notice us. Your sister, Jessica. Little Miss Perfect, Elizabeth Stupid Wakefield!"

Stupid! Jessica felt her stomach muscles tense. "Don't call my sister stupid," she said. "She may be a lot of things, but she isn't stupid." *And anyway, I'm the only one who's allowed to call her that!* "And you don't have any proof that she took those things," she argued.

"Proof, schmoof!" Bruce said scornfully.

"Of course she did it, Jessica." Lila stepped forward. "Who needs proof? She's done everything else. Why not this?"

"Because—because—" *Because the Elizabeth I know wouldn't do anything to harm anybody,* she thought. *Ever!*

"Because it just isn't like Elizabeth," she said at last.

Janet gave a heavy sigh. "You're her sister, Jessica," she said. "We wouldn't expect you to understand." She flashed a meaningful glance at Lila and Mandy.

"What do you mean?" Jessica felt a surge of irritation. "What do you mean, I wouldn't understand?"

"Just what I said." Janet raised her arms and let them drop. "Perhaps we shouldn't even be talking to you anymore. I mean, if those losers at the other end of the island have a *spy* among us—" Lowering her head, she said something to Lila that Jessica didn't catch.

"I think we should reconsider membership qualifications for the club if this keeps up," Lila announced, stealing a quick glance at Jessica.

"I think we should reconsider whether certain people belong on this end of the island at all," Bruce said frostily.

Jessica's mouth dropped open. *They can't be serious!* Her mind raced. "I was only wondering—" she began, her tongue feeling like a block of wood.

"Yeah, right." Janet laughed contemptuously. "Look. Either you're with us—"

"Or you're against us," Lila finished for her.

Jessica laughed nervously. "Um—" *Of course I'm on your side,* she thought. *I just don't know that Elizabeth is capable of —*

"Tell us right now, Jessica." Bruce's voice sounded stern.

Jessica gulped. *This is no kind of a choice at all,* she thought miserably, looking around at all the angry faces staring at her. *I can't let them say these horrible things about Elizabeth!*

"What's it gonna be?" Bruce barked.

"Stay—or go?" Janet added, a sparkle in her eye.

But I can't risk being kicked out of the Unicorns, either! Quickly Jessica thought over all the terrible things Elizabeth had ever done to her. The day Elizabeth "borrowed" her nail polish and spilled it on Jessica's homework. *Yes.* Jessica found herself balling her hands into fists. All the times when Jessica sat in the backseat of the car while Elizabeth got to sit in the front. *I mean, when she* forced *me to sit in the back.* She breathed deeply. *When Elizabeth beats me at Monopoly. And isn't sorry about it afterward, either! And when she bugs me about putting the cap back on the toothpaste—and calls the Unicorns the Snob Squad—and—and—*

"Today!" Bruce yelled.

And sabotaging the raft. Yeah, it's totally possible—I mean, likely—that she did sabotage it! Jessica looked up at him, her eyes blazing. "You're absolutely right," she said, surprised how easy it was to convince herself of Elizabeth's guilt. "I'm with you."

"All right, Jessica!" Lila applauded.

Jessica breathed a sigh of relief. She tried to ignore the churning feeling in her stomach. *What if we're wrong?* a voice in her head asked. She shook her head firmly, hoping to silence the voice. *What Bruce said made sense,* she told herself.

After all, who else could have taken the fruit?

"This is so weird," Cammi said a little later that morning. "I was positive I put all our shoes right here." She pointed to a rock at the edge of the pool. "I lined them all up just before bed, and now they're—gone." Her eyes cast anxiously around the pool.

Elizabeth could feel her stomach sinking out from under her. *Just what we need,* she thought. "I guess it's OK as long as we stay on the beach," she said slowly, looking out to sea. *Looks like storm clouds out there,* she thought.

"But there aren't any fruit trees on the beach," Randy said. He winced as he looked off into the forest, where the ground was littered with sticks and thorny twigs. "I don't like the idea of going in there barefoot. Not without a first-aid kit."

Elizabeth shuddered. She had to agree with him.

"But how could they have disappeared?" Cammi asked. She stared once more at the empty rock, as if willing the shoes to come back.

"Wild animals?" Amy suggested, twirling a lock of hair around her pinky.

Maria shook her head. "Animals don't wear shoes, and they don't eat them, either."

"My dog chews on them," Cammi said uncertainly.

Maria laughed. "There were too many shoes for it to be wild animals. Anybody else have an idea?" She glanced around the circle of kids.

Elizabeth raised her hand slowly. "Maybe the tide washed them away."

"Couldn't be." Randy shook his head. "We were sleeping on the beach below this rock. If the tide had come this far up, we'd all have been washed out to sea."

Elizabeth wrinkled her brow and tried to think. But she couldn't come up with any other answers—except one she didn't want to think about.

Todd cleared his throat. "Let's face it," he said. "We all know what really happened last night, don't we? Bruce and his group came back and stole our shoes. Just to bug us." His voice began to rise. "Agreed?"

"But we don't *know* that," Elizabeth protested, even though Todd's words had a terrible ring of truth to them.

"No other solution fits the available evidence," Randy pointed out.

"I'm sorry." Maria patted Elizabeth's shoulder. "But with friends like those—"

"This is getting really annoying," Amy muttered.

"It's not just annoying, it's dangerous!" Todd exclaimed. "It's a good thing we collected a bunch of fruit yesterday. And *hid* it." He sighed loudly. "I'd almost rather be stranded with the hijackers than with those clowns."

"I just don't think—" Elizabeth's voice faltered. "I just don't believe Jessica would do such a thing."

"Well, believe it," Todd told her firmly. He looked up at the sky as the clouds closed in overhead. "We'd better get under the roof before it begins to pour. Good thing we made that thatched cover the other day." He started down the beach.

With a heavy heart, Elizabeth followed along. *There has to be another explanation,* she thought. *I don't believe Jessica would—* A raindrop hit her forehead. She glanced up at the gray sky as the rain began to spatter down.

"Run!" Amy commanded. She darted across the beach, leaving little footprints in the moistened sand.

Elizabeth covered her head with her sweatshirt and followed. The rain was really pouring now. She could see little holes in the sand where the droplets were landing. *I'll be happy to get dry,* she thought, feeling almost glad that Jessica's group was gone. *No way we could all have fit under that cover.* Water began to drip down her nose. She ducked her head and ran faster. *Only a few more yards—*

"Hey!"

Startled, Elizabeth looked up. Todd and Maria were standing between two trees, soaking wet. "What's going on?" she asked, wiping raindrops out of her eyes. *Rain goggles with windshield wipers,* she told herself. *That's what someone should invent.* "What—?"

With an enraged look on her face, Maria pointed upward.

The branches of the tree, the rain clouds— Elizabeth squinted. *Wait a minute!* "It's gone!" she shouted, turning to Maria in alarm. "The shelter is gone!"

"Tell me about it," Maria said over the sound of the pelting raindrops. She held out her dripping arms. "So, is this wild animals, Elizabeth? Or tides?" Lowering her head, she and the others dashed for the tunnel, leaving Elizabeth alone on the beach.

Elizabeth's mind flashed back to the expression on Bruce's face after the raft had broken. *Yes,* she thought as the water ran down her legs, *I know who's responsible for this.* She was suddenly convinced that Bruce would do anything to bother her and her friends. *I could have seen it in Bruce's eyes, if I only hadn't been trying so hard to pretend that we could all work together.*

"Aren't you coming, Elizabeth?" Maria's voice floated back through the rain.

Elizabeth pictured Jessica and her Unicorn friends, warm and dry beneath their thatched roof. *Our thatched roof,* Elizabeth corrected herself, remembering who had actually built it. It was a terrible image, one that chilled Elizabeth to the bottom of her heart. She hated believing that her own sister would do something so horrible. Or that she would stand by while her friends did.

But there weren't any other explanations. *Those Unicorns,* she thought miserably. *A thatched roof—and extra shoes in case their own get wet!*

She ran to catch up to Maria, doing her best to hold back her tears of rage and disappointment.

I wish I had some dry clothes, Jessica thought miserably. *And a dry pair of shoes!* She and her friends were huddling beneath a palm frond. Rain pounded her head and joined little rivers rushing around her feet. There had to be enough water in her shoes to quench the thirst of everyone in Los Angeles.

For a week!

"I'd give anything for that thatched roof," she heard Bruce growl from the other side of the tree.

"It was ours just as much as theirs," Lila agreed.

"More ours, really." Aaron joined the conversation. "I mean, they used some of our sticks and vines."

Jessica wiped some extra water out of her lap. It didn't seem to make her any drier. "I'd give all my Johnny Buck CDs for a big towel right about now," she grumbled. A picture of Elizabeth and her friends, warm and dry beneath the thatched roof, forced its way into Jessica's mind. She imagined her sister sitting back happily, and Amy or Maria saying something stupid to her. Something like, "Do you think this rain will ever stop?" And Elizabeth saying, "Gee, I hope not! Not as long as Bruce and those dumb Unicorns are out in it!" *And then they'd giggle hysterically,* Jessica told herself. *Maybe they'd even sing some stupid song. What's that one from Winnie-the-Pooh? "And the rain, rain, rain came down, down, down . . ."*

She wanted to feel angry with her sister. *No, not just angry. Furious!* But somehow she couldn't make it work. She was feeling sadness as much as anger—maybe even more. *I guess I really believed*

Elizabeth wasn't capable of mean tricks, she thought.

"Doesn't it just make you want to barf to think about them all warm and dry?" Lila was saying crossly.

"You bet," Jessica said as fiercely as she could. Still, it was no use. Thinking about Elizabeth sabotaging the raft just made her feel miserable. And lonely, too. Lonely for the real Elizabeth, her wonderful, exasperating twin, who did nice things. And who really loved her. Or used to, anyway.

"And the rain, rain, rain came down, down, down—"

In a sheltered lagoon not far from where Elizabeth had found the briefcases, two figures sat warm and dry beneath a thatched roof. Next to them was a pile of fresh fruit, which Jessica and her friends would have found awfully familiar. And next to the fruit was a pile of tennis shoes, which Elizabeth and her friends would have found awfully familiar, too.

No one was watching as one of the figures added a log to the crackling fire. But any of the kids on the island would have recognized those men right away.

"And the rain, rain, rain came down, down, down," the man called Jack sang again in a mocking baritone. He stopped and gave a rough laugh. "But not on us, huh? Just on all those little Piglets out there."

"It's like taking candy from babies," his friend Gary said, patting the pile of tennis shoes beside him. Gary was a huge, barrel-chested man with beady eyes and hair the color of wet sand.

Jack laughed again. Jack was smaller than Gary,

but not much. His hair was messy and dark, and his eyes were menacing. "You said it," he agreed. "They sleep so soundly." Picking up a piece of fruit, he bit into it with a crunch. "Yummy, yummy. Thanks, kids."

"Guess they need their beauty rest or something," Gary added. He glanced at the rain pelting down outside their stolen shelter. "So it's settled."

"You bet," Jack said quietly. "First, we take our money back."

Gary reached across the fire. The two men shook hands and sat back again.

"And then?" Jack asked, his lips curling into an enormous, lopsided grin.

"Then we do what we should have done back there on the boat." Gary's eyes glittered.

Jack leaned forward. "And then?"

"Then we kill those kids."

Nine

The rain had stopped, but Jessica's shoes still squeaked as she strode purposefully through the forest. "How can Elizabeth do this to me?" she said to no one in particular, clenching her teeth. "I mean, after all we've been through together—"

"Yeah, really," Aaron muttered, pushing his wet hair off his forehead. "And after she acted like she wanted us to work together."

"Well, we're not going to let them get away with it," Janet said fiercely.

"What if they give us a hard time?" Lila wanted to know.

"Then we take *our* shelter back, that's all there is to it," Bruce snapped. "And the fruit they stole from us. And anything else we can find. Hey, after all the trouble they've caused us, we ought to take their stupid tennis shoes off their stupid feet!"

Jessica splashed across the stream. It seemed

deeper than yesterday. Her feet disappeared well past her ankles. *Oh, Elizabeth,* she thought wistfully, looking down at her sodden shoes. *How could you let your own twin sister get so wet?*

"So who's going to do the talking?" Mandy asked as the group hurried along.

"I will," Jessica and Bruce said together.

They looked at each other, and Bruce lifted an eyebrow. "I'm the leader of this group," he told her firmly.

"Maybe," Jessica replied, just as firmly. "But she's *my* sister."

"I don't think I've ever been so wet in my entire life." Maria groaned, wringing water out of her shirt.

"Me neither," Todd sighed. He shook himself like a dog coming out of a lake. Water sprayed in all directions. "What I wouldn't give for a hair dryer right about now."

"I know what you mean." Cammi stepped out of the tunnel and gave a little half smile. "At least the rain has stopped."

"I hope those other kids enjoyed the shelter that they didn't help make," Amy said sarcastically. "I hope they're nice and warm and dry. Pfft!" She stuck out her tongue and blew hard toward the other side of the island.

Elizabeth was seething. As angry as her friends were, she knew that none of them could be as angry as she was. "Personally, I hope they drowned!" she burst out. "I've been wetter, but I've never been madder! I mean, the nerve! The pure, stupid"—she groped for words—"selfishness of those kids!"

Maria and Amy stared at her in shock.

"Wow," Maria said softly. "I don't think I've ever heard you sound like that."

"I'm furious!" Elizabeth said, biting her lip till it hurt. "I'm furious with that know-it-all Bruce, and I'm furious with that bossy Janet, and I'm furious with that silly old Lila, and—" She paused.

And I'm furious because they've taken Jessica away from me.

"If I could just get Jessica alone, even for a minute," Elizabeth murmured. She was surprised at how lost and lonely she felt without her sister nearby. Quickly she looked up the hillside. "There's a path. Come on!"

Elizabeth dashed to a break in the rocks. Soon the others were following her.

"Where are we going?" Maria asked as Elizabeth led the way up the path.

"To find them, of course," Elizabeth said, already breathing hard from the climb. "Wherever they are, I'm going to find them, and I'm going to get our shelter back." She winced as she stepped on a stinging nettle. "Not to mention our shoes."

"I'm with you," Todd said, swinging his way up the path behind her.

"Me too." Amy followed along.

"We'll tell them their little game is over," Elizabeth said, blinking in the sunlight as she climbed. Little thorns stuck her in the heel, but she did her best to ignore them. "We'll tell them that we're sick and tired of this nonsense." She scampered up to the top of the hill and raised her voice so everyone could hear her. "We'll tell them—" She searched her mind for a good comparison. "We'll tell them King Kong is more civilized than they are. We'll tell them—"

"You'll tell us what?"

Elizabeth looked up. A familiar face was standing on top of the hill, blocking her path. *Jessica*. Elizabeth hadn't expected to see her sister quite so soon. She wetted her lips and looked nervously at her friends.

"What exactly were you planning to tell us?" Jessica's voice was sharp and mocking. She glanced at Bruce and the others in her group. "Because," she added with exaggerated politeness, "if you can't think of anything to say—" Her eyes flashed. "Then we've got some things to say to you."

"Yeah, like, thanks a lot for the tricks," Lila said spitefully. "Just because Bruce has all the good ideas doesn't mean you have to steal our food."

"Steal your food?" Maria came up behind Elizabeth's shoulder. "We didn't steal your food!"

"Yeah, right," Bruce said, rolling his eyes in disgust.

"We have plenty of our own!" Randy insisted. "And we don't even know where you guys are camping out."

"A likely story." Aaron took a step forward.

"Yes, very likely!" Elizabeth had found her voice at last. No way was she letting Jessica and her friends intimidate her. She spoke up firmly, hoping she wouldn't stutter. "And besides," she challenged Jessica, "how about our shoes? Why don't you just hand them over?"

"Fun's fun," Maria chimed in, "but this is just plain stupid."

"Shoes?" Jessica stared at her sister, confusion written all over her face. "What shoes?"

"You know perfectly well what shoes," Elizabeth countered, her voice rising. *Why don't you just admit it!* she wanted to cry. She longed to forgive her sister and be friends again. But she felt much too hurt and betrayed to be nice. "The shoes that aren't on our feet! The shoes you stole when we were asleep."

Maria narrowed her eyes. "And then there's the little matter of the shelter you stole from us last night."

"Last night?" Jessica interrupted. "Oh, last *night*. You mean while you guys were over at our camp stealing our food." She took a step toward Elizabeth.

Elizabeth took a step forward, too. *I could actually strangle Jessica,* she told herself. The idea was strangely disgusting and fascinating at the same time. She could feel her hands taking on a life of their own. It was all she could do to keep them at her sides. "I don't think you should talk like that," she said through clenched teeth.

"I'll say whatever I please," Jessica replied, tossing her head.

"Just get off this island!" Elizabeth whispered, her heart beating furiously. She tried to add something even more threatening, but all she could manage was a whispered "Please?"

"I would if I could!" Jessica hissed back. "But thanks to you—" She stepped forward once more. Now the two sisters were almost jaw to jaw. "Why don't you just get your ugly face out of my life, huh?"

"Look who's talking," Elizabeth said, struggling to keep her composure. "In case you've forgotten, you and I look exactly alike. So whatever you say about my face, you're saying about your own, too."

"Ha," Jessica said. "I'm much more beautiful than you are. And you know it."

Elizabeth was about to respond when she heard a noise beside her. She swung around to look. There stood Cammi, pebbles dropping from her hand—

And a scream coming from her mouth.

"What is it?" Jessica demanded, her heart fluttering. She tore her eyes away from her sister. *Cammi,* she thought with contempt. *One of Them.*

Cammi fell silent. Quivering, she pointed out to sea.

Jessica looked into the distance. "There's nothing there," she said. *Rats.* She'd hoped maybe it was a ship. Still, it figured that one of Elizabeth's stupid friends would go around screaming for no good reason. She was turning back to Elizabeth when something else caught her eye. Something on the beach below the hill.

"That's where we found the money," Elizabeth whispered. All the fight seemed to have gone out of her voice. Jessica shoved her aside impatiently and went to the edge of the hillside. She drew in her breath.

Etched carefully into the smooth, damp sand, in letters about eight feet high, was a message.

"A dollar sign," Jessica murmured, squinting to make sure she wasn't seeing things. Her eyes flicked over the rest of the writing. "OR YOU ARE—"

Oh, man. Nervously Jessica licked her lips. "OR YOU ARE DEAD," she finished, feeling as though she'd just been socked in the stomach. Her gaze bounced back and forth along the stretch of sand. But except for a few footprints around the letters, the beach was completely empty.

"We didn't do that," Elizabeth said, in a voice scarcely above a whisper. She turned to Jessica. "And you couldn't have, either." She swallowed hard. "We both got here just after it stopped raining. Whoever made that did it after the rain stopped. Or else the rain would have washed it away."

Fear seized Jessica's heart. "So—"

"Hold on." Bruce pushed his way forward. "Are you all here?" He counted Elizabeth's friends. Then he gave a low whistle. "Sorry. I thought maybe—"

"No," Elizabeth said, shaking her head. "We're all here. We've all been here."

"Oh, man," Jessica said aloud this time. She stared at Elizabeth, her eyes wide and her heart pounding. "So—" But she couldn't get the words out.

So who put the message there?

It's like Robinson Crusoe, Elizabeth thought numbly, remembering the famous story of the man who was shipwrecked on an island. *He thought he was all alone, and then one day he saw a footprint in the sand. Just a single footprint, but—* She gulped.

But it was enough to tell him that he was not alone.

"So who put those words there?" she asked aloud, aware of how helpless her voice must sound. In the story, she remembered, the footprint had belonged to a man called Friday. Friday had become Robinson's helper and friend.

Somehow, Elizabeth doubted that this message was made by a friend. She looked out over the beach, suddenly wanting to forget where she was, to ignore what was happening. She stared off at the blue-green water beyond. Little whitecaps sparkled in the afternoon sun, and far out to sea Elizabeth could just make out a family of dolphins playing happily in the salty water. *A family of dolphins,* Elizabeth thought with a pang. Suddenly she missed her mother and father more than she could ever remember missing them.

"Pirates maybe?" Maria guessed in a weak voice. She looked pleadingly at Elizabeth. "The message talks about money."

"It's not pirates, Maria," she heard Mandy saying.

"I guess—I guess I kind of knew that," Maria answered shakily.

Bruce looked around. "All right," he said. His voice sounded flat and harsh. "Let's not beat around the bush. We all know who wrote that, don't we?"

Elizabeth slowly nodded. *It's the men who can't possibly be here,* she thought, a shiver snaking its way down her spine. *The men who tried to kill us once already—the men who couldn't have escaped from the sinking ferryboat.*

Couldn't—but did.

She breathed deeply and squeezed her eyes shut tight.

The hijackers!

Ten

"They're going to find us," Lila said, her voice rising in panic. "They'll find us, and then they'll torture us, and—"

Jessica tore her gaze from the message on the beach below them and reached for a stick. "No, they won't, Lila."

"They will, they will, they will." Lila gasped. "They almost killed us once on the boat, and then they tried to kill us again, and now—"

Maria walked over and shook Lila roughly. "Stop it! They won't find us."

"Yes, they will," Randy spoke up. "We've been all over the island."

"So we'll hide," Jessica said, clutching her stick tightly. *At least the hijackers don't have any guns,* she thought, remembering how they'd tossed the robbers' guns overboard before the boat sank on Saturday . . . four days ago. *Was it really four days?* she thought. *Unbelievable.*

"It won't do any good." Randy spoke slowly but firmly. "We've left tracks everywhere."

"The rain washed them all away!" Maria pointed out triumphantly. "As long as we stay here—"

"We've left melon rinds," Randy continued. "We've set up two camps. We've made a ton of noise—"

Randy's right, Jessica realized, looking at the ground. Her throat felt tight. "Then it must have been the hijackers who were playing those tricks last night," she said, squeezing the words out.

Elizabeth looked startled. "You're right!" she said in a half whisper. "I should have known." She touched Jessica's long blond hair, which was only now beginning to dry in the sunshine. "Your hair was way too wet for someone who'd been hiding under a thatched roof. Oh, Jess—" Elizabeth's face twisted up, and for a moment Jessica thought her sister was about to cry. "I'm sorry. I—I should have known it wasn't, you know, your fault."

Jessica felt a rush of relief. She gave her sister a small smile, but somehow it didn't seem like the time or the place for tearful reunions. "Um—don't worry about it," she said thickly. "So—what now?"

No one said a word. Jessica could almost hear the seconds ticking away.

"We've got to hide," Bruce said at last. Licking his lips, he stared at the message once more. "Do you—do you think they know we have the money?"

"I think so." Jessica read the message again. A thought struck her. "Hey! Do you think—maybe—if we give them the money, maybe they won't bother us?"

"You don't really believe that." Janet's voice oozed with disapproval.

"Well—" Jessica waved her arm at the message below. "It says, 'dollar sign *or* you die.' If we give them the money, maybe they'll be satisfied and go away. I mean, it doesn't say 'money *and* you die.'" She studied the faces of the other kids. "After all—" Her voice broke. "It isn't exactly our money."

"No, but it's the only thing keeping us alive," Elizabeth said fearfully. "Don't you see? They don't know where it's hidden. They won't kill us until they get the money—because if they kill us all, they'll never find it."

"Elizabeth's right," Aaron said. "Remember how many times they tried to kill us on board the *Island Dreamer*?" He shuddered. "I don't trust them."

"Besides," Amy pointed out, "even if we did give them the money, how would they get off the island? By building a raft?"

"Listen." Elizabeth sounded suddenly decisive. "Listen up, everybody. Let's tell them that only one of us knows where the money is hidden—but that we'll never tell which one. As long as they don't know where the money is, they'll keep us alive. They won't take a chance on killing the only one who knows."

"That sounds good," Jessica said, reaching for her sister's hand.

I only hope it works, she thought, staring down at the beach. *I only hope it works!*

"So are we all agreed?" Elizabeth asked, looking anxiously around the circle of kids in front of her.

"Only one person knows where the money is, and we'll never tell who. It's our only chance."

Next to her, Aaron nodded slowly. "That makes some sense," he said. "What do you think, Mandy?"

Elizabeth took a deep breath as she watched Mandy consider the question. "I'll go along with it," Mandy said at last.

"Good," Elizabeth said. *Aaron, Mandy, and Jessica,* she thought. It looked like a good chunk of Bruce's crowd. "Is there—"

"Nice try, *Queen* Elizabeth!" Bruce put his hands on his hips and faced Elizabeth. "But since when do you make all the rules around here?" He looked meaningfully at Janet.

"Yeah, that money is everyone's business," Janet contributed. "You have no right to make decisions for me!"

"Really," Lila agreed.

Elizabeth stared at Bruce, her mouth open. "I didn't mean to sound bossy," she said, wondering if she had sounded that way. *Of all the times to argue over who's in charge—*

"Maybe you didn't *mean* to," Bruce went on, "but you did. You're not junking me as leader just because—"

"Who said you were leader?" Amy snapped.

"He's a much better leader than Elizabeth would ever be!" Lila said loyally.

Maria pointed an accusing finger at Bruce. "You're just jealous because Elizabeth had a good idea and you didn't."

"Ha!" Bruce laughed mockingly. "I can't help it if she's bossy."

"Can't you think of something besides being in charge, just for once?" Todd demanded.

Elizabeth looked anxiously at Jessica. She had a horrible feeling that she knew what was about to happen.

"This has nothing to do with who's in charge, Wilkins," Bruce said. "The problem with Elizabeth's idea is that, um—"

"That the hijackers would never believe us," Janet finished.

"Yeah." Bruce nodded. "And also, *we're* going to hide so we'll *never* be found." He waved his hand in the air. "The trouble with you, Wakefield, is that you're a loser. You're thinking about *when* they catch us. That's a loser's way to look at it. Right, Dallas?" His voice had a sharp edge as he stared at Aaron.

"Um—right," Aaron said uncertainly.

"Jessica agrees with us, too," Janet went on, glaring in Jessica's direction. "Unicorns always stick together. Don't you agree, Jessica?"

Jessica gulped. "Um—" she began.

"Well, Lila, what do you suggest?" Elizabeth interrupted quickly, not wanting to hear her sister's answer.

"Ask *Bruce*," Lila replied. "*He* knows."

Elizabeth shook her head. She didn't like the way this conversation was going. "Seriously, guys, we've all got to stick together, or—" She twisted her hands. "It's our only chance."

"Now where have I heard that before?" Janet asked, curling her lip in disgust.

"Well, let's see," Bruce said, pretending to tick things off on his fingers. "First, there was 'we have to stay next to the waterfall.' Then there was 'we have to put the money where *I* tell you to.' Then there was—"

"That wasn't me!" Elizabeth cried. "That was *your* idea—"

"Just get a life, Elizabeth," Lila interrupted with a snort.

Elizabeth tugged at her hair in frustration. "I think—"

"Well, don't!" Janet commanded. "Who cares what you think, anyway? Just listen to Bruce for once in your life!"

"Yeah, well, we did that already," Todd exclaimed. "And look what happened! The raft totally fell apart, and Elizabeth almost drowned."

"We all know why that raft fell apart," Bruce snarled, glaring at Elizabeth.

Elizabeth looked desperately from Todd to Bruce. "I thought we'd just decided that it was the *hijackers* who wrecked the raft."

"Yeah, well," Lila said, waving her hand dismissively. "If you'd let us make that SOS we'd all be home by now!"

Elizabeth let out a loud groan. Suddenly, she couldn't take it anymore. "Can't we stop arguing?" she pleaded.

But it was too late. Janet was already storming off into the bushes, followed by Lila, Bruce, Aaron, Mandy—and, after a moment of hesitation, Jessica.

Elizabeth's heart sank. *Oh, Jess,* she thought sadly, shaking her head. "Divide and conquer," she muttered under her breath. *What a silly, silly argument. An argument over nothing—nothing at all.*

Well. She sighed heavily. Maybe they really were better off in two small groups than in one large cluster.

But somehow, she doubted it.

"All right." Jessica looked expectantly at her friends. *What a dumb argument that was,* she found herself thinking. *Elizabeth's idea was a pretty good one, actually.* Elizabeth's ideas usually were, she had to admit. She hoped they hadn't made a serious mistake. "Where should we hide?"

"Down near the water, I guess." Bruce stuck his hands in his pockets.

"It's kind of open down there," Mandy objected. "They'd see us really easily."

"But we could see them first," Jessica pointed out. "I vote for the beach."

Mandy shook her head. "If we stay in the forest, they'll never find us."

Everybody looked at Bruce.

"Mandy's right," Bruce said without much conviction. "Let's stay in the forest."

Jessica felt a nervous twinge in her stomach. She remembered a game of cops and robbers she'd played at Lila's house one day last year. She'd walked around and around the mansion, up and down stairwells, past closed doors, never knowing when someone was about to jump out at her, never knowing when someone might be sneaking up on her from behind.

Even now, Jessica could feel a shiver. "I'm going to the beach," she announced, her voice a little unsteady, her stomach tying itself into knots.

"Aw, Jess!" Aaron made a face.

"You should come, too," she informed him. "If you stay in the forest, you'll wake up tomorrow morning with your throat slashed. They'll sneak up and you'll never know they're coming." She swallowed hard. "But if you come down to the beach, you just might survive. You choose!"

Aaron's face darkened. "Throat slashed?" he repeated.

Jessica nodded gravely.

"OK. I guess I'm with you," Aaron said in a small voice.

Bruce cleared his throat. "Well, I guess we could all go to the beach. I mean, I wouldn't feel right leaving you two there alone." He squared his shoulders importantly. "That wouldn't be the responsible thing to do."

Jessica rolled her eyes and led the way down to a rocky section of the shore. To her left, Jessica could see the coastline curve around, covered by several rock formations. To the right lay a sandy beach. Jessica took a quick look at the beach and heaved a sigh of relief. *No footprints.*

"Where?" Janet demanded, shivering. "I don't like standing out here where they can see me."

"In one of the little caves, I guess," Jessica said. She looked to Bruce for support. "Which one do you think, Bruce?"

"Um—" Bruce looked around vaguely. "How about there?" He pointed to a covered grotto right down by the water's edge. Jessica could see little holes in the sides of the rock. "Watchtowers," she murmured.

"OK by me," Aaron agreed. "We can post guards."

Jessica nodded. *This just might work,* she thought, allowing herself to feel hopeful for the first time in a while. She examined the sides of the rocky grotto as the kids squeezed through the narrow entrance. Outside she could hear the rhythm of the waves and the single voice of a lonesome sandpiper.

Aaron and Jessica took up positions at the tiny "windows" while the others huddled together on the floor. Jessica stared out across the sand. She shifted her body farther to the right. "Oh, man," she muttered, just loudly enough to be heard. "I'd forgotten our footprints."

"Our footprints?" Mandy looked up questioningly.

How could we be so stupid? "Our footprints," Jessica repeated. "When we walked across the beach to get here. The sand's still wet enough for our tracks to show up. Anyone who walks nearby will know we're in here."

"Oh, no!" Lila whimpered from the floor of the grotto.

Bruce took a deep breath. "It's low tide right now," he whispered. "At least, I think so. The tide'll come in soon. Maybe it'll wash the footprints away."

Jessica nodded, though she was doubtful. Some of the footprints seemed pretty far up the beach. "I hope you're right, Bruce," she said grimly, clutching what remained of her broken stick.

Oh, boy—do I ever!

"Quietly now," Amy said, holding up a warning finger to her lips.

Elizabeth didn't know how much longer she could stand all this walking—especially barefoot.

But what alternative did they have? They had to get as far away from their camp as they could, and they had to make sure they left no tracks that could be followed.

"Wow," Amy said suddenly, coming to the edge of a steep cliff. Quickly she stepped back and peered down. Elizabeth looked, too. *We've got to be thirty feet up,* she thought. *It's steep but not too steep to climb down.* Then she blinked. *What's that?*

Elizabeth stared into a bluish lagoon surrounded by palm and cypress trees. To her left the trees formed a perfect semicircle, marking the boundary of the lagoon. To her right, a narrow passage led out to the open sea. And in the middle—

A dinghy, Elizabeth thought in amazement. She rubbed her eyes. It was too good to be true. *A boat!*

"Yes!" Todd exclaimed. He pumped his arms up into the clear air.

"Awesome," Amy whispered, staring down into the lagoon. A small smile began to crinkle across her face. "We're free."

The dinghy had oars, Elizabeth saw to her delight. She measured the size of the boat with her eyes. *Uh-huh. It should be plenty big for all of us.* "That must be how the hijackers got here," she murmured. "And if we're lucky, it won't be how they leave."

Randy grinned at her. "Let's get out of here," he suggested, groping for a foothold on the rocky cliff.

"Last one down is a rotten egg!" Maria called.

Elizabeth drew a deep breath. "Aren't you forgetting something?" she asked.

"Well, a map and compass sure would be nice,

but what can you do?" Maria teased Elizabeth. "Hey, this is freedom staring us right in the face. It's our only chance—as someone I know likes to say." She tugged Elizabeth's sleeve. "C'mon. Race you down."

Elizabeth was tempted, but she held firm. "We can't," she said, wiping her forehead. "What about the others?"

"The others?" Maria looked blank.

"They wouldn't wait for us," Cammi argued. "Come on, let's go."

"No." Elizabeth suspected that Cammi was right. *But it doesn't make any difference,* she told herself sternly. *My sister's on this island, and even if she and her friends are all creeps, I can't leave them.* "We have to rescue them, too," she said aloud.

Randy frowned. "Really, Elizabeth, I think our best bet is to get help from a fishing boat or something."

Elizabeth shook her head. "We have to get them off, too. Go if you like—but I'm not coming!"

For long moments she just stared at her friends. Finally Amy stepped forward. "You're right, Elizabeth. We can't just leave them."

Maria's face softened. "No—I guess we can't."

"But we should hurry up and find the others," Todd added.

Elizabeth grinned, a rush of warmth flooding through her. "Compared to everything else we've done this trip, that should be a breeze!"

Some great hiding place, Jessica thought bitterly an hour later. Her feet were soaking wet once again. For that matter, her ankles were soaked, too.

Not to mention her shins and her knees.

"You sure were right, Jessica," Janet said sarcastically, standing nearly waist-deep in a pool of water. "You said the tide would come in, and what do you know, it did." She eyed Jessica scathingly. "Of course, the water's not only going to wash the footprints away, it's going to wash us away, too."

Jessica grit her teeth. *It was Bruce who said the tide might come in,* she thought, but she didn't say anything. She tried to lift her leg to drier ground. Little ripples spread out from her knee and lapped against the fringes of Lila's shorts.

"Jessica!" Lila glared across the grotto.

Mandy's forehead creased with worry. "I hate to be a wet blanket, but I'm wondering how high this tide will get," she said. "I mean, if we wait much longer the whole entrance to the cave could be under water."

"She's right," Bruce said. "We have to make a run for it. Who's first?"

"Not on your life!" Lila gasped.

"I'll go," Jessica volunteered. "Anything's better than this." She sloshed her way over to the entrance to the grotto. *I hope there aren't any crabs hanging on the rocks,* she thought as she squeezed through the narrow passage. *Some great hiding place!* Behind her she could hear Aaron start to come through the entrance.

Let's see, Jessica thought, wondering which direction to head next. At the other end of the beach she could see another, bigger grotto, with bigger windows and farther from the ocean. *If we wade through the water we shouldn't leave any footprints,* she thought. *And if we can make it there without being seen—ow!*

At that moment, a pair of hands grabbed her roughly and threw her to the ground. Her broken stick flew out of her hands and onto the sand, where it landed with a dull thump.

"Hey!" Jessica tried to yell, but the words wouldn't come out. A hand clamped itself over her mouth and pressed hard. It smelled of fish and melons, and Jessica started to gag. The next thing she knew, she was lying half in and half out of the water, her hands tied firmly behind her. Looking up, her heart beating wildly, she stared straight into the familiar face of Gary, the hijacker.

"So we meet again," he told her, giving her a mock bow. "But this time, the pleasure is all mine." His beady eyes seemed to bore right into her face.

Jessica swiveled her body around. Next to her lay Aaron, tied with thick vines, just as she was.

She swallowed hard. The hopelessness of their situation came to her in a rush.

They were caught.

And there wasn't a thing they could do about it.

Eleven

The vines cut painfully into Jessica's wrists as she staggered through the forest. *It's hard to walk when your arms are tied to other people's,* she thought, fighting a sense of panic.

Especially when those other people are named Lila and Janet!

"Get a move on!" the hijacker named Gary commanded.

A mulish look appeared on Lila's face. "I can't," she protested. "I think these vines are cutting off the circulation in my arms."

"Oh, I see," Jack said with phony concern. "And you walk on your arms, huh?" He gave Lila a push, sending her body crashing against a tree.

"Oooof!" Lila tumbled to the ground, dragging half the line with her.

Caught off guard, Jessica landed in a heap on top of her. "Ow!" she cried. *I will never take my arms for granted again,* she promised herself as she wobbled back up, pushing on Lila's body for support. *Cross my heart and hope to die!*

"If you've broken my ankle, you're going to be in big trouble," Lila proclaimed from the ground. "My father knows lots of really good lawyers. He'll sue you for everything you've got."

"She's right." Janet's eyes flashed. "*My* father knows someone who broke an ankle when a cement mixer fell on her at a football game. *She* sued and got three billion dollars. Or something like that."

"Oh, I'm so scared," Gary squeaked, kicking Lila until she stood upright again. "Three billion dollars! Gee, Jack, do we have that much in our piggy banks?"

"Let's count our pennies as soon as we get home!" Jack said. "And speaking of money," he added, a menacing tone creeping into his voice, "maybe you'd like to tell us what you kids did with the money you found, huh?"

Her heart thumping, Jessica turned to face the hijackers. "The money we found? Gee, guys, you must be mistaken," she said bravely. "We didn't find any money—did we, Mandy?"

"No way," Mandy agreed.

"I might have a couple of nickels in my pocket," Jessica continued. "You can have that, I guess, if you want money so badly."

"We're really telling the truth, sir," Aaron said earnestly as they stepped out onto the beach by the waterfall. "Really. Promise."

And we actually are telling the truth, Jessica thought, suppressing a grin. *Elizabeth and Maria were the ones who found the money—not us!*

"Hmm." Gary frowned with concern.

"Cross our hearts and hope to die!" Janet said loudly.

"Yeah, we didn't see any five million dollars or anything like that," Lila added in a firm voice. "Uh-uh. No way."

Gary stiffened. "You didn't what?" he asked, staring at her curiously.

Oh, Lila. Jessica groaned in her mind as Lila went pale.

"Just where was this money you didn't see?" Gary asked Lila.

Lila gulped and looked at the ground.

Gary flashed another look at Jack. "And the money was all inside, um, a big cardboard box, right?" he said, stroking his chin. "I mean, a shoe box, sorry. A box with 'Nike' written across the top, am I right?"

Lila jerked her head up. "Of course not, you idiot!" she said, glaring at Gary. "It was in two big briefcases—"

Jessica's heart dropped. *That does it,* she thought with dread.

The corners of Gary's mouth crinkled up into a wicked grin. "Oldest trick in the book," he said at last. "Thanks, kid. You're a star!"

"I'm—making it up," Lila sputtered.

Jessica shook her head in dismay. Now *she figures it out,* she thought.

"So. Where's the money?" Jack demanded. He brushed his dark hair out of his eyes. "You can tell us now—"

"Or," Gary interrupted, "you can tell us later." He

drew his forefinger across his throat and made a gurgling sound.

No one said a word.

Jessica's throat felt tight from thirst, but she decided to ignore it. Suddenly she realized that they had only one choice. *It's now or never,* she thought. *Elizabeth's idea makes sense. We have to try it. Only one of us knows, and we're not telling which one—maybe they won't kill us then.*

She opened her mouth to speak, and then closed it. She glanced at her friends, all lashed together with the strong vines from the forest.

What if they get mad at me? She tried to swallow. *Bruce is desperate to be in charge, and Janet—*

Jessica paused and licked her dry lips. *I have to say it,* she ordered herself. *I have to! No matter what Janet and Bruce think. If Janet kicks me out of the Unicorns, well, so what? We'll probably be dead anyway.*

She took a deep breath. "You can't scare us." Her voice sounded oddly thin. "Only one of us knows where the money is hidden. And we're not telling which one it is."

There was silence. Jessica stared at her feet, scared to see the looks on the faces of her friends.

Gary prodded Bruce with his toe. "She right, kid?"

Bruce looked at the ground. Jessica held her breath. *Please, Bruce . . .*

Licking his lips nervously, Bruce started to say something, but his voice caught.

"Speak up!" Gary demanded, thrusting Bruce's head back. "We can't hear you!"

Bruce cleared his throat and spoke firmly. "Like she said. Only one of us knows, and we're not telling who!"

Yes! If Jessica's arms hadn't been tied, she would have pumped them into the air with delight. *All right, Bruce!*

She stole a glance at Gary. He was staring at Bruce through narrowed, hateful eyes. "OK," he said sharply. "Everybody sit down on the beach."

Jessica dropped down to the warm sand. She was getting thirstier by the second, but it felt good to sit. She did her best not to glance toward the tunnel where the money was hidden. It was tough to keep a secret when the secret was so close by!

"See, we can wait," Jack said in a surprisingly gentle voice. He picked up a melon rind, which Jessica figured was left over from last night's dinner, and filled it with clear water from the pool. Then he held it out toward the kids, a glint in his eye. "Anyone like some water?"

Me, Jessica thought, realizing how hot it was out in the sun. Her tongue felt dry and swollen. She tried to figure out when she'd last had something to drink. The water in the rind looked very tempting.

"I would!" Lila sang out.

Jack stared at her, the beginnings of a smile playing over his face. "Oh, yeah?" he asked. "Well, you'll get some. As soon as we get our money."

Jessica tried to look away as Jack poured the cool, clear liquid over his face and into his throat. She licked her chapped lips.

How long can a person live without water? she wondered dismally.

"You don't even know where they're hiding," Randy challenged Elizabeth as she led the way across the island. "This is a complete wild-goose chase!"

"Randy's right, Elizabeth," Maria added gently. "If the hijackers can't find them, there's no way we will."

Elizabeth grimaced as a thorny branch raked her forearm. "We'll find them," she said, hoping she sounded more confident than she felt. They had been walking for what seemed like hours, though Elizabeth suspected it hadn't been much more than twenty minutes.

"It's not too late," Randy argued, reaching to grab Elizabeth's sleeve. "We can turn around and take the dinghy."

"And leave Jess here? No way!" Elizabeth quickened her pace. There was something up ahead on the beach—something familiar.

"Jessica!" she cried, breaking into a run. Her twin was in clear view between the trees, sitting quietly on the beach. *Sunbathing?* Elizabeth briefly wondered what on earth Jessica thought she was doing, lying in the sun with two hijackers loose on the island, but it didn't seem to matter. "Jess!"

Jessica looked up. For a split second Elizabeth caught an expression of unimaginable terror on her sister's face.

"Go back, go back!" she could hear Jessica shouting. "Run!"

What in the world? Elizabeth didn't slow down as she careened past the waterfall and onto the beach. "Jessica!" she shouted once more.

"Oh, Elizabeth." Jessica looked as if she might cry.

Elizabeth backed away in alarm. *Something's wrong.* Her eyes darted around her. *Something's going on.* The other kids were sitting too quietly—and where were Jessica's hands, anyway?—and why was there a vine lying out in the middle of the beach?

She was still wondering when a hairy arm reached out and knocked her onto the sand.

"So where's the money?" Jack's eyes bored in on Elizabeth. She squirmed on the sand. In what seemed like seconds, the hijackers had tied her and her friends up with vines. Now they sat on the sand, as helpless as Jessica and the others.

Jack kicked a little sand in Elizabeth's face. A few grains got into her eyes. "Well?" he barked.

Elizabeth squeezed her eyes shut against the sand. "I—well—"

"I told you guys already," Bruce interrupted. "Only one of us knows—and we're not telling who."

Elizabeth glanced at him with surprise. Of all people to take her advice!

"You might as well let us go," Bruce went on, "because we're not going to cooperate with—yuck!" He spat out a mouthful of sand.

Gary stood above Bruce, grinning hugely. "Listen, guys," he said in a low voice. "No one wants to see you get hurt, OK?"

Elizabeth rolled her eyes. *Yeah, right*, she thought.

"So we'll make you an offer," Gary said, plastering a smile onto his face.

"Soooo—what do we have for the kiddies, Gary?" Jack asked, opening his eyes as wide as he could and showing his stained teeth.

"Well, Jack," Gary chirped, waving his arms this way and that, "the first prize is an all-expenses-paid, completely free, vaaaay-cation!"

"Oooh!" Jack exclaimed.

"Ahhh!" Gary agreed, clapping wildly. "The lucky winner will travel in high style aboard a lifeboat stolen from that amazing ship, the *Islaaaand Dreamer!*"

"Oooh!" Jack said again.

Elizabeth fought back her tears. *They're about to kill us, and they're pretending they're on some dumb game show!*

"Before the ship sank, of course," Gary went on. "The winner gets a free trip for one to the beautiful town of Sweet Valley, Caliiiii-fornia!"

"Ahhh!" Jack jumped up and down. "What can these kiddies do to win, Gary?"

"That's the greatest part!" Gary yelled. "They don't got to dress up in stupid costumes! They don't got to know the presidents or any of that jazz! They don't got to roll dice or spin spinners!" He raised his arms over his head. "All they got to do is—"

"Give us our money," Jack finished grimly, looking down the row of kids. "Well?"

No one spoke.

"It's a real nice prize, Gary," Jack said at last, folding his arms across his chest. "Be a shame to let it go to waste."

"It sure would," Gary agreed, approaching Todd. "How about it, kid?"

Tell him off, Todd, Elizabeth begged.

"Over my dead body," Todd spat out.

Gary nodded. "Over your dead body," he repeated slowly. "Well, kid," he added with a nasty little laugh, "you wait. You just may get your wish."

* * *

"So." Jack's voice was rough. "We kill one every hour till someone tells us where the money is hidden."

"Sounds good to me," Gary agreed.

The sun was going down. Jessica wondered vaguely whether she would ever see it rise again. Next to her she could hear Lila whimpering. "Hang on, Lila," she whispered, sliding over a little closer to her friend. "You can do it."

"I'm so thirsty." Lila moaned.

"I know." Jessica's own throat felt as dry and dusty as a fire. "We'll get you something to drink. Soon. I promise." But how she was going to carry out that promise, Jessica didn't have a clue.

"I can't hold out much longer." Lila's voice was scratchy.

"Don't you dare tell," she hissed as the first stars appeared in the sky overhead. "If you tell, I'll—I'll—" She racked her brain for an appropriate punishment. "I'll kill you."

Lila moaned again, a little louder this time.

"Want some water?" Gary asked gently, appearing at Lila's side with a melon full of liquid. "Nice and cool."

"Uh-uh," Jessica mouthed to Lila, shaking her head violently.

"You're onto something, Gar," Jack called out, watching the scene from the pool. "She just might be the one. The kid next to her is telling her to shut up!"

Alarmed, Jessica snapped her mouth closed.

"Beautiful fresh water," Gary hummed.

Jessica drew in her breath, fighting her own urge to cry out for the water.

"Um—I don't know," Lila said slowly, her voice breaking. "I'm—so thirsty."

"Sure, sure," Gary said soothingly. "There's plenty of water here. We'll even untie you!" He leaned closer to Lila, close enough for Jessica to smell the salt on his body. "Just tell us where the money is—OK?"

"Um—" Lila began helplessly. "Um—"

Jessica couldn't stand any more. "Knock it off!" she demanded. "She doesn't know anything—anything at all." Her voice sounded thin and chalky in the twilight.

"That's right," Aaron chimed in. "She's not the one. We promise."

"But—" Lila said, beginning to cry. Jessica was frantically searching her brain for another way to distract the hijackers, when she heard a voice she hadn't heard in a while—a voice from the other end of the chain.

"Excuse me—sir?" Bruce asked.

"Yeah?" Gary stood back up, away from Lila. "What is it, kid?"

There was a moment's silence. In the darkness, Jessica strained her ears to hear.

Bruce took a deep breath. "I think I'm ready to cut a deal with you," he said in a small voice.

Twelve

Tears stung Elizabeth's eyes as she listened to Bruce talking to the hijackers. *He's really serious,* she thought hollowly. *He's really going to do it.*

Elizabeth swallowed hard. Of course, it made sense that a selfish, obnoxious creep like Bruce would be the one to save his own skin—and sacrifice everyone else. *I should have known it was too good to be true when he told them only one of us knew. I should never have trusted him.*

Next to her she could hear Mandy beginning to whimper. *Maybe they won't actually kill us,* she thought, a faint glimmer of hope in her heart. *Maybe they'll just be happy with the money, and they'll leave us here.*

"And we won't even make you watch while we kill your friends and dump 'em in the ocean," Gary was saying to Bruce. "How's that?"

"It's very kind of you, sir," Bruce said softly.

Elizabeth lay on the ground and turned her face

away from Bruce. *What a rat,* she thought. *What a rat.* Her thoughts turned to her family. Her mother—her father—Jessica. She thought of family cookouts in the backyard . . . card games around the dining room table . . . bike rides on soft spring afternoons . . . making fudge with Jessica after school . . .

It can't be all over now, she thought miserably. *It just can't.*

That's strange, Jessica thought, leaning forward as far as the vines around her wrists would allow. She tuned out the whimpers and cries around her and focused on what Bruce was saying.

"The money's in a cave," she heard him tell Gary. "We walk up that hill a little ways." He pointed. "The entrance is just around the other side."

"OK," Gary growled. He tugged Bruce to his feet. "Show us."

What's he talking about? Jessica wondered. *The money's in a tunnel, not a cave. And the easiest entrance to reach is right here by the waterfall.*

"Let's go." Jack pushed Bruce roughly in front of him. "Man, we're going to be rich," he said exultantly. "How far to the cave, kid?"

"Just a couple of minutes," Bruce replied.

Jack pumped his arm. "Two more minutes and we're rolling in the dough. Then we'll take care of the rest of you."

Jessica's mind raced. She'd been hoping they'd forget all about her and her friends—but she'd suspected all along that they wouldn't. Her mouth felt drier than ever. *Two minutes there, two back—just four more minutes to stay alive.*

She willed her heart to stop pounding. *Every moment counts,* she thought wildly as the blood raced through her temples. *Every single second!* Glancing around frantically, she saw no help anywhere—she saw nothing at all but the faint glow of the burning piece of wood that would light the hijackers' way to the money.

"I just want to say good-bye to my friends," Bruce said shyly. Unwillingly, Jessica looked up to see Bruce silhouetted against the starry sky. Gary held one of his arms, Jack the other. *The nerve!* she thought angrily. *First he sacrifices us—then he wants to say good-bye!*

"I'm really sorry I have to do this to you." Bruce spoke slowly, as though reading from a script. "It wasn't, like, my first choice or anything."

Yeah, sure, Jessica thought scornfully. But she didn't want him to stop talking. Every second that he spoke meant another second of life.

"But they exerted undue pressure on me," Bruce continued, staring down into the shadows toward Jessica and her friends.

"Enough!" Gary pushed Bruce forward. "Let's get out of here!"

"Not!" Bruce cried out as the hijackers pulled him over the top of the hill. Jessica watched in despair. All around her there was complete silence, except for the steady roar of the waterfall.

I can't believe him, Elizabeth thought, scared and angry at the same time. *"They exerted undue pressure on me." Here he is, sacrificing his friends, and he's talking like a stupid college professor. Undue pressure—yeah, right!*

Something tugged at her brain. *Wait a minute.*

Elizabeth sat up sharply, the vines cutting into her wrists. *That's not how Bruce talks,* she told herself. *Randy, sure. But certainly not Bruce!*

The words "undue pressure" echoed and re-echoed in Elizabeth's mind. "Undue," she said slowly to herself, tasting the way it felt on her tongue. "Undue pressure." *And then what did he say?* "Not!" she said aloud.

"Huh?" Mandy stared at her, her eyes red-rimmed from crying.

"Sssh!" Elizabeth shut her own eyes tight. "Undue—pressure—not," she whispered. "Undue—" It was on the tip of her tongue. "Undue—not!" Elizabeth's heart gave a little leap. *Of course!* She re-spelled the words in her mind. "'Undue—not' becomes 'undo—knot!'" *Undo the knots!* With the crooks gone for a couple of minutes, they could untie each other's ropes and maybe—just maybe—stand a fighting chance! "Give me your wrists!" she hissed at Mandy, rolling as close to her as possible.

"What?" Mandy looked up.

"Your wrists," Elizabeth hissed again. With her own fingers she groped behind her. *Mandy's elbow—lower—lower—ah.* Her thumb brushed the knot that held Mandy's arms together. "I'm going to untie this," she told Mandy, trying desperately to stay calm, praying the hijackers wouldn't come back too soon.

"I think it's—right about—here." Bruce slowed his pace and stooped. *Ouch,* he thought, feeling a twinge in his arm. He frowned up at Gary. *You don't have to pull my elbow off!* But he didn't dare say anything.

"Right here?" Jack leaned over and peered at the ground. "You sure?"

"Sure I'm sure," Bruce told him. He kicked the grass with his toe. "See? There's a hole that leads to the—um, cave."

"OK." Jack aimed the burning stick downward. "You first, Gary."

Gary released his grip on Bruce's arm. *Thanks, buddy,* Bruce thought sarcastically, rubbing his elbow.

The three of them dropped into the pit. The burning stick cast ghostly shadows in the darkness. "Um—why don't you let me hold that," Bruce suggested, swallowing hard. "The—the, um, exact place is kind of hard to see."

"What'd you do—bury it under a rock?" Gary asked with a low growl.

"Something like that," Bruce replied, taking the stick from Jack's hands. His palms were sweaty. The tunnel was a much eerier place at night than it was during the daytime. No rays of light shined through the ceiling. Except for the torch, the cavern was completely dark. *I hope this works,* he thought, taking a step forward.

"No tricks, now," Gary warned him.

"Oh, no, sir," Bruce said, shaking his head as he inched forward. Three steps, four steps, five. Out of the corner of his eye he could see the rock where they'd set the briefcases. Forcing himself to look away from it, he counted another three steps beyond.

"Hey!" Jack's voice sounded brittle in the darkness. "How far back does this cave go, anyway?"

"Not much farther," Bruce lied, hoping he sounded convincing. "I think we're almost at the back of it now." *Two more steps—three—far enough!*

"What gives?" Gary asked, his fingers digging into Bruce's elbow. "Why did you stop?" Nervously he cast his eyes around the cavern. "I don't see nothing."

Bruce gave a low whistle. "Stupid of me!" he said. "We went too far. Let me take a couple of steps back and I'll—"

Gary grunted and turned Bruce around. "Where?" he demanded, the word sounding like an explosion.

Stay calm, stay calm, Bruce told himself, walking slowly forward. "Right—about—here!" He kicked aside the rock that concealed the briefcases.

"Yes!" The sound of Gary's yell echoed through the chamber. He released Bruce's elbow and dropped to the ground, his fingers scrabbling against the clasps of the nearest case.

Jack chortled as Gary pulled out the bag. "Empty it," he directed. "I want to touch the stuff."

"We're rich!" Gary shouted, tearing the plastic and flinging crisp new hundred-dollar bills into the air.

"Millionaire City, here we come!" Jack dumped the money onto the dry leaves that covered the floor of the cavern. "Oh, man, I never thought I'd see the day!"

Bruce stepped slowly back, deeper into the tunnel, raising the burning stick higher and higher. *Keep it up,* he urged them silently. *Come on, come on—pour the other one out, too.*

Gary held the second briefcase open as Jack spilled the money out onto the ground. Bruce tensed his muscles. Suddenly his elbow didn't hurt so much anymore. *Another few seconds.*

Jack riffled through a handful of bills. Bruce

could hear a crackling noise, like a box of cereal being torn open. "Oh, man, oh, man!" Jack began, pressing the bills to his lips. Bruce felt his heart thunder in his chest. It was time.

Stepping forward, he lifted the stick into the air like a spear. It etched a blazing trail through the tunnel and over the robbers' heads. Then, in a swift movement, Bruce brought it down—right on the pile of dry, brittle money.

There was a sizzling sound, and flames suddenly leaped up from the floor of the tunnel.

"Hey!" Gary jumped up in alarm and swung around. "Hey, kid!"

But he was too late. Bruce was gone.

Thirteen

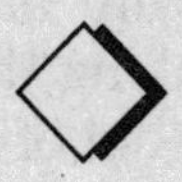

"Hurry—hurry—" Jessica begged, her heart in her mouth.

Elizabeth knelt behind her, her fingers fumbling with Jessica's knots. "Hold still!" she commanded, peering forward in the darkness.

"I am!" Jessica bit her lip. All around her she could see other kids springing up, free at last from the vine ropes that had held them so long.

Elizabeth pulled out the last loop. "There you go!" she said happily.

Jessica rubbed one wrist hard, hoping the flow of blood hadn't been cut off too long. Her fingers tingled.

"Why don't you help Maria?" Elizabeth asked. "I'll take care of Lila."

Undoing Maria's knots turned out to be harder than Jessica expected. Her fingers, still stiff from hours of not moving, weren't doing what she wanted them to.

"What's that?" Maria suddenly sat straight up and squinted through the darkness. "There's a light." Jessica followed her eyes—and gasped.

"It's not a light," she said, panic rising in her throat. On the far side of the hill, flames were shooting high into the night sky. "It's a fire!"

"No!" Maria stared at Jessica.

"It's coming from the place where Bruce led the hijackers," Jessica said with alarm. She pulled Maria quickly to her feet, yanking the last knot loose as she did so. "We'd better get out of here," she said urgently.

"Everybody to the dinghy!" Elizabeth commanded.

Jessica stared at her sister. "The dinghy?" she repeated.

"There's a dinghy across the island," Maria explained quickly to Jessica. "We found it when we were running from the hijackers."

"Really?" Jessica couldn't believe her ears. "Then why didn't you—why are you—" She swallowed. "I mean—"

"Because Elizabeth insisted on saving you and your friends," Maria said. "Come on. We'd better get going." Still holding the vine, she took a few tentative steps forward.

Jessica felt a rush of warmth. *My sister could have escaped—and instead she came back to get me!* She felt incredibly guilty for having treated her sister so shabbily. *Here I was accusing her of all these rotten tricks,* she told herself, *and all the time Elizabeth was doing the most awesomely loyal and wonderful thing in the world—saving my life!*

As kids scampered toward the forest, Elizabeth placed a hand on Jessica's arm. "We've got to save

Bruce," she said. "He doesn't know about the lifeboat."

"Forget Bruce!" Jessica cried out angrily, but even as she spoke she knew she didn't mean it. *Elizabeth's right,* she thought, kicking the ground in front of her. *She wouldn't leave without me—and we can't leave without Bruce.*

There was a sudden movement next to the waterfall. Jessica spun around as a dark figure flew through the blinding spray and crashed down into the pool below. With a gasp, Jessica recognized him. *Bruce.*

Jessica didn't stop to think twice. With Elizabeth at her side, she waded out into the pool and seized Bruce by the shoulders. "It's shallow," she told him, helping him upright. "What's going on?"

Bruce's breaths came in great shuddering gasps. "The money's on fire!" he blurted out. "I blocked the tunnel entrance—on the other side—with fire—and—"

"Take it easy," Jessica told him, helping him into the forest. "So the hijackers are trapped in the tunnel?"

"Don't know." Bruce spit out some water. "Maybe—or maybe they ran through the fire. They might have—come after me." He stumbled forward in the darkness. "We got to—get out of here."

"We will," Elizabeth said assuredly. "We're heading for a dinghy we know about. No, don't ask," she added quickly as Bruce made a wheezing noise somewhere deep in his throat. "We'll tell you all about it—when we're safe."

Jessica bit her lip. She looked around the dark forest. *Does Elizabeth know which way we're going?* she wondered.

And can we make it to the dinghy before the crooks find us?

And what about the fire?

Jessica shook away her fears and helped Bruce over a root. "When we're safe," she repeated.

"Hurry, hurry!" Cammi urged Lila. Behind them the flames crackled ominously. "The island could go up in smoke any minute!"

"I can't!" Lila was in tears. She hobbled along next to Todd, in obvious pain. "I just tripped on a rock, and I think I twisted my ankle!"

"OK." Cammi slowed her pace. She reached across Lila's back for Todd's hand. "We'll make you a human chair. Lean back—"

"Like this?" Lila fell heavily against their arms.

"Something like that." Cammi placed her other hand behind Lila's knees and grabbed Todd's wrist. "One—two—three." Groaning, she and Todd lifted Lila as Lila wrapped her arms protectively around their shoulders.

"Ready?" Todd asked, stealing a frightened look back at the flames.

Cammi nodded. "Let's go!"

"Oh, no," Amy sobbed. A humongous fallen tree was blocking the path ahead.

Aaron sucked in his breath. He looked quickly over his shoulder. *No hijackers yet,* he told himself.

"I think we can get over it," Randy said. He tried to find a foothold but fell back onto the ground. "Oooof!"

Aaron measured the log with his eyes. "I don't think so," he said, shaking his head. "It's just too big—unless—"

"Unless what?" Amy asked.

"Unless we help each other," Aaron said. He cupped his hands and held them out to Randy. "Come on, Mason. I'll give you a boost, and then it's up and over."

Aaron grunted as Randy stepped into his outstretched hands.

"Got it!" Randy's voice crowed in triumph.

"OK, Amy, you're next." Aaron helped Amy jump into his hands.

"Just like Boosters," Amy said, managing a half grin.

"Reach out your arm, Dallas," Randy called from the top of the tree.

Aaron frowned, then shook his head. "No," he said firmly, looking over his shoulder. "There are still more kids behind us. They'll need help getting over." He swallowed hard. "I'm staying here."

"We're there," Elizabeth breathed. She stood at the top of the cliff, looking down into the cove where the boat was waiting.

"It looks kind of steep," Janet said doubtfully, leaning over the edge. "I don't know if—"

"You'll make it, Janet," Maria said firmly. "Promise."

"I know!" Mandy snapped her fingers. "Let's make a human chain."

"How about Lila?" Cammi demanded, setting the injured girl onto the ground. "We'll have to get her down somehow." Lila whimpered with pain.

"I know!" Elizabeth turned toward Maria, who was still carrying the vine the thugs had tied around her hands. "We'll tie one end around Lila, and a couple of us can lower her down slowly, while someone walks below and makes sure she doesn't fall. All right?"

"Brilliant, Wakefield," Bruce said, clapping her on the back. "But we'd better hurry. I think I hear them coming now!"

"Everybody aboard?" Jessica shouted a few minutes later.

"I think so." Mandy looked pale.

On the edge of the cliff, two figures appeared. *Or is it only my imagination?* Jessica hoped fervently that it was only her imagination. "Go!" she cried frantically.

With a grunt, Elizabeth and Bruce ran forward, shoving the boat off from the shore. Maria reached out to help Bruce on the boat.

Jessica watched happily as Janet helped Elizabeth climb over the rail. "We're off!" she cried.

Cammi stroked the water with one oar while Aaron took the other. They rowed in perfect unison, steering the dinghy out of the narrow cove and into the open sea.

Jessica stared back into the forest. The sight was breathtaking. The fire blazed on one corner of the island, sending sparks shooting up into the sky and obscuring even the brightest stars. Jessica watched in amazement as the smooth water shimmered in beautiful shades of red and gold.

Elizabeth slid over and squeezed Jessica's hand. "It's beautiful, isn't it?" she whispered.

"You mean what we're seeing?" Jessica whispered back. "Or the fact that we're safely off the island?"

"Both, I guess," Elizabeth said, smiling.

Jessica grinned and reached out to fluff her sister's hair. "You know what?" she asked softly.

"What?" Elizabeth leaned a little closer.

"You need a shower," she said, giving her twin a hug.

Fourteen

"Ahoy there!"

Elizabeth dropped her oar in surprise. She'd been rowing for only a few minutes, and now a fishing boat was looming out of the darkness toward them.

"People have been looking for you for days," the captain of the boat said, staring down into the small lifeboat. "You're the school group that got hijacked, aren't you?"

"That's right," Elizabeth said, letting the dinghy drift up against the fishing boat.

"Are you all right?" the captain asked. A rope ladder came flying over the edge of the fishing boat. Todd caught it expertly and held it while Janet began the climb up.

"We're fine," Elizabeth called back up. A twinge of disappointment hit her. Part of her had wanted to row home. *And the way we've been working together, I think we could have,* she told herself.

Still, she had to admit she was just as happy to be rescued.

Elizabeth scampered up the ladder. At the top the captain's face greeted her. "We picked up the captain of the *Island Dreamer* a couple of days back, along with his first mate," he told her.

"You did?" Elizabeth asked, letting out a sigh of relief. "I'm so glad. Are they—" She paused. "Are they OK?"

"Just fine. They told us the whole story up to the time they were set adrift." The captain of the fishing boat stared hard at Elizabeth. "You haven't been in that little lifeboat the whole time, have you?"

"Well, um, not exactly," Elizabeth told him.

The captain looked at her curiously. "What have you been doing, then?"

A million thoughts flashed through Elizabeth's mind. Gathering fruit, exploring the tunnel, the arguments on the beach, the briefcases full of money, the warning on the sand, even their missing tennis shoes. She smiled up at the captain.

"You'd never believe me if I told you," she said, shaking her head.

"Jessica! Elizabeth!"

The dock at the Sweet Valley Marina was jammed as the fishing boat steamed in early the next morning. "I see Mom and Dad," Jessica told Elizabeth, staring through the crowd. Her heart leaped. She couldn't remember the last time she'd been so glad to see them.

"Not to mention—" Elizabeth began.

"Our wonderful brother." Jessica sighed. Then she

smiled despite herself. *I'm even glad to see Steven again.*

The boat came to a shuddering stop against the dock. Jessica was off like a rocket. "Mom!" she cried, dashing off down the gangplank with Elizabeth only a few steps behind. "Dad!"

Mrs. Wakefield swept both girls up into the biggest hug Jessica had ever gotten. "Oh, Mom," she sighed.

Steven hovered nearby. "Glad to see you kids," he said offhandedly. "Hey, next time you get stranded on a desert island, make sure there's a pay phone on the beach, OK?"

"Same to you, Steven," Jessica told him, smiling. She realized she'd even missed his teasing.

"We're so glad you're safe," Mrs. Wakefield murmured.

"We sure are," Mr. Wakefield agreed.

Jessica grinned at Elizabeth, who grinned back. Beside her she could see the other kids greeting their parents. Her heart swelled. *We did it,* she thought. *We had our differences, our arguments, but when we needed to work together, we did!*

"They actually look like they're in pretty good shape, don't they?" The captain of the fishing boat stopped by and ruffled Jessica's hair. "How'd you do it?"

The twins exchanged glances. "Teamwork," they told him at the same exact moment.

"I knew it!" Jessica exclaimed from the doorway of Elizabeth's bedroom that night after dinner.

Elizabeth looked up from her book. "You knew what?"

"I knew you'd be flopped on your bed exactly like that, reading that exact Amanda Howard mystery," Jessica said triumphantly.

Elizabeth laughed. "A pretty good guess, Jessica, considering I always read in this position when I'm tired and you knew I was planning on reading this book after I finished the last one."

Jessica tossed her hair. "Yeah, well, how was I supposed to know you'd finished the last book?" She tapped her forehead with her finger. "I'm telling you, Elizabeth, I get more and more proof all the time."

"Proof of what?" Elizabeth asked suspiciously.

"That I'm psychic, of course," Jessica replied.

Elizabeth rolled her eyes. "Jess, we've been through this before. . . ."

"Yeah, well, I'm tired of no one believing me," Jessica said with a frown. "I'm going to prove I'm psychic once and for all!"

***Is Jessica really psychic? Find out in Sweet Valley Twins #93,* The Incredible Madame Jessica.**

Bantam Books in the SWEET VALLEY TWINS series.
Ask your bookseller for the books you have missed.

- #1 BEST FRIENDS
- #2 TEACHER'S PET
- #3 THE HAUNTED HOUSE
- #4 CHOOSING SIDES
- #5 SNEAKING OUT
- #6 THE NEW GIRL
- #7 THREE'S A CROWD
- #8 FIRST PLACE
- #9 AGAINST THE RULES
- #10 ONE OF THE GANG
- #11 BURIED TREASURE
- #12 KEEPING SECRETS
- #13 STRETCHING THE TRUTH
- #14 TUG OF WAR
- #15 THE OLDER BOY
- #16 SECOND BEST
- #17 BOYS AGAINST GIRLS
- #18 CENTER OF ATTENTION
- #19 THE BULLY
- #20 PLAYING HOOKY
- #21 LEFT BEHIND
- #22 OUT OF PLACE
- #23 CLAIM TO FAME
- #24 JUMPING TO CONCLUSIONS
- #25 STANDING OUT
- #26 TAKING CHARGE
- #27 TEAMWORK
- #28 APRIL FOOL!
- #29 JESSICA AND THE BRAT ATTACK
- #30 PRINCESS ELIZABETH
- #31 JESSICA'S BAD IDEA
- #32 JESSICA ON STAGE
- #33 ELIZABETH'S NEW HERO
- #34 JESSICA, THE ROCK STAR
- #35 AMY'S PEN PAL
- #36 MARY IS MISSING
- #37 THE WAR BETWEEN THE TWINS
- #38 LOIS STRIKES BACK
- #39 JESSICA AND THE MONEY MIX-UP
- #40 DANNY MEANS TROUBLE
- #41 THE TWINS GET CAUGHT
- #42 JESSICA'S SECRET
- #43 ELIZABETH'S FIRST KISS
- #44 AMY MOVES IN

Sweet Valley Twins Super Editions

- #1 THE CLASS TRIP
- #2 HOLIDAY MISCHIEF
- #3 THE BIG CAMP SECRET
- #4 THE UNICORNS GO HAWAIIAN
- #5 LILA'S SECRET VALENTINE

Sweet Valley Twins Super Chiller Editions

- #1 THE CHRISTMAS GHOST
- #2 THE GHOST IN THE GRAVEYARD
- #3 THE CARNIVAL GHOST
- #4 THE GHOST IN THE BELL TOWER
- #5 THE CURSE OF THE RUBY NECKLACE
- #6 THE CURSE OF THE GOLDEN HEART
- #7 THE HAUNTED BURIAL GROUND
- #8 THE SECRET OF THE MAGIC PEN
- #9 EVIL ELIZABETH

Sweet Valley Twins Magna Editions

THE MAGIC CHRISTMAS
BIG FOR CHRISTMAS
A CHRISTMAS WITHOUT ELIZABETH

#45 LUCY TAKES THE REINS
#46 MADEMOISELLE JESSICA
#47 JESSICA'S NEW LOOK
#48 MANDY MILLER FIGHTS BACK
#49 THE TWINS' LITTLE SISTER
#50 JESSICA AND THE SECRET STAR
#51 ELIZABETH THE IMPOSSIBLE
#52 BOOSTER BOYCOTT
#53 THE SLIME THAT ATE SWEET VALLEY
#54 THE BIG PARTY WEEKEND
#55 BROOKE AND HER ROCK-STAR MOM
#56 THE WAKEFIELDS STRIKE IT RICH
#57 BIG BROTHER'S IN LOVE!
#58 ELIZABETH AND THE ORPHANS
#59 BARNYARD BATTLE
#60 CIAO, SWEET VALLEY!
#61 JESSICA THE NERD
#62 SARAH'S DAD AND SOPHIA'S MOM
#63 POOR LILA!
#64 THE CHARM SCHOOL MYSTERY
#65 PATTY'S LAST DANCE
#66 THE GREAT BOYFRIEND SWITCH
#67 JESSICA THE THIEF
#68 THE MIDDLE SCHOOL GETS MARRIED
#69 WON'T SOMEONE HELP ANNA?
#70 PSYCHIC SISTERS
#71 JESSICA SAVES THE TREES
#72 THE LOVE POTION
#73 LILA'S MUSIC VIDEO
#74 ELIZABETH THE HERO
#75 JESSICA AND THE EARTHQUAKE
#76 YOURS FOR A DAY
#77 TODD RUNS AWAY
#78 STEVEN THE ZOMBIE
#79 JESSICA'S BLIND DATE
#80 THE GOSSIP WAR
#81 ROBBERY AT THE MALL
#82 STEVEN'S ENEMY
#83 AMY'S SECRET SISTER
#84 ROMEO AND 2 JULIETS
#85 ELIZABETH THE SEVENTH-GRADER
#86 IT CAN'T HAPPEN HERE
#87 THE MOTHER-DAUGHTER SWITCH
#88 STEVEN GETS EVEN
#89 JESSICA'S COOKIE DISASTER
#90 THE COUSIN WAR
#91 DEADLY VOYAGE
#92 ESCAPE FROM TERROR ISLAND

SIGN UP FOR THE SWEET VALLEY HIGH® FAN CLUB!

Hey, girls! Get all the gossip on Sweet Valley High's® most popular teenagers when you join our fantastic Fan Club! As a member, you'll get all of this really cool stuff:

- Membership Card with your own personal Fan Club ID number
- A Sweet Valley High® Secret Treasure Box
- Sweet Valley High® Stationery
- Official Fan Club Pencil (for secret note writing!)
- Three Bookmarks
- A "Members Only" Door Hanger
- Two Skeins of J. & P. Coats® Embroidery Floss with flower barrette instruction leaflet
- Two editions of *The Oracle* newsletter
- Plus exclusive Sweet Valley High® product offers, special savings, contests, and much more!

- - - - - - - - - - - - - - - - - - - -

Be the first to find out what Jessica & Elizabeth Wakefield are up to by joining the Sweet Valley High® Fan Club for the one-year membership fee of only $6.25 each for U.S. residents, $8.25 for Canadian residents (U.S. currency). Includes shipping & handling.

Send a check or money order (do not send cash) made payable to "Sweet Valley High® Fan Club" along with this form to:

SWEET VALLEY HIGH® FAN CLUB, BOX 3919-B, SCHAUMBURG, IL 60168-3919

NAME ______________________________________
(Please print clearly)

ADDRESS ______________________________________

CITY ____________________ STATE ________ ZIP ____________
(Required)

AGE ____________ BIRTHDAY ________ / ________ / ________

Offer good while supplies last. Allow 6-8 weeks after check clearance for delivery. Addresses without ZIP codes cannot be honored. Offer good in USA & Canada only. Void where prohibited by law.

LCI-1383-123